# *Praise for Alison Kent!*

"For me Alison Kent's name on a book means
that I am guaranteed to have a story
that is realistic, entertaining, compelling
and sexy as all get-out."
—ARomanceReview.com

"Alison Kent has created in her giRL-gEAR
series a believable, modern world where men
and women behave just a little bit naughtier
than they do in real life."
—AllAboutRomance.com

"An outstanding tale of passion, sensuality
and a dark fascination, Ms. Kent's romance
turns up the heat."
—*Romantic Times BOOKreviews* on
*The Sweetest Taboo*

"Alison Kent delivers a knockout read."
—*Romantic Times BOOKreviews* on *All Tied Up*

"Alison Kent mesmerizes us with a compelling
love story brimming with scorching sensuality
and abiding love."
—*Romantic Times BOOKreviews* on *Call Me*

# Blaze™

Dear Reader,

I am a pop culture junkie. Not an addict, mind you. Or overly obsessive. I do love hearing who has landed plum movie roles, finding out what television series are canceled or renewed, seeing unexpected guest stars show up on network TV, etc. But I don't wait for news on celebrity Starbucks sightings, or even care much about the love lives of the stars. Still, I know that's not the case with everyone.

Funnily enough, I created the character of Caleb McGregor—aka Max Savage—long before *stalkarazzi* shows were as popular as they now are, but I'm glad I waited until the age of YouTube and TMZ to write his romance with Miranda Kelly, aka Candy Cane. Having one of them dreading the impending bombardment of the media and making the other one an expert at doing the bombarding made the story great fun to write.

I hope you get a kick out of Caleb and Miranda as they kiss and tell, kiss and don't tell, then don't kiss and tell some more! You can e-mail me at ak@alisonkent.com to let me know if you do. Stop by my blog at www.alisonkent.com/blog to visit with other readers and lovers of Harlequin Blaze, and to win all sorts of books and fun prizes. I'll see you again in March 2009, when I'll be hitting the track for Blaze's 0—60 miniseries.

All my best,

*Alison Kent*

# ALISON KENT
## Kiss & Tell

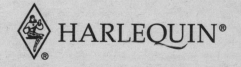

HARLEQUIN®

TORONTO • NEW YORK • LONDON
AMSTERDAM • PARIS • SYDNEY • HAMBURG
STOCKHOLM • ATHENS • TOKYO • MILAN • MADRID
PRAGUE • WARSAW • BUDAPEST • AUCKLAND

ISBN-13: 978-0-373-79433-1
ISBN-10:    0-373-79433-9

KISS & TELL

www.eHarlequin.com

**Printed in U.S.A.**

## ABOUT THE AUTHOR

Alison Kent is the author of five sexy books for Harlequin Temptation, including *Call Me*, which she sold live on CBS *48 Hours*, several steamy books for Harlequin Blaze, including *The Sweetest Taboo* and *Kiss & Makeup*, both Waldenbooks bestsellers, a number of sizzling books for Kensington Brava, including the Smithson Group series, as well as a handful of fun and sassy stories for other imprints. She is also the author of *The Complete Idiot's Guide to Writing Erotic Romance*. Alison lives in a Houston, Texas, suburb with her own romance hero.

## Books by Alison Kent
### HARLEQUIN BLAZE

To Walt, for TMZ
To Brenda, for Dumbledore
To HelenKay, for making sure I stayed sane

# Prologue

*April…*

"AN APPELLATE RULING has paved the way for a retrial in the case of Baltimore businessman E. Marshall Gordon. The CEO of EMG Enterprises was the fifth member of the board of directors to face charges of conspiracy to commit fraud related to EMG's off-the-book partnerships. More on that in our national news segment after the break.

"And coming up in our celebrity beat, we have the latest from Max Savage on Colorado congressman Teddy Eagleton's recent divorce from his wife of twelve years, and his romantic connection to Ravyn Black, the lead singer of the chart-topping emo band Evermore—"

"Enough, already." Corinne Sparks reached to flip off the small television set she kept in the back room at Under the Mistletoe, almost knocking over a glass vase of hyacinths and lilies as she did.

Miranda Kelly, Corinne's employer and owner of the flower shop in the resort town of Mistletoe, Colorado, had been seconds from doing the same thing. Neither one of them enjoyed seeing pieces of their lives on the news, and to be mentioned that way, one on top of the other—first her ex-husband, then Corinne's estranged daughter—was too much.

"Tell me about it." Miranda had been intent on using the quiet spring day for bookkeeping, but the specter of her past impinging on her present allowed room for little else in her head. "I left Baltimore so I wouldn't have to be bombarded by the media's obsession with everything related to Marshall. I sure don't want to think about him while I'm paying bills."

Frowning, Corinne resituated two of the lilies that had slipped in the close call. "I thought you left because the SOB couldn't keep his zipper zipped."

*Well, there was that,* thought Miranda, swiveling on the bar stool she used at the short end of the long L-shaped worktable that served as a desk. "That's why I divorced him. And seeing his face every time I turn on the news these days reminds me how stupid I was to marry him in the first place."

"He wasn't a cheater when you married him," Corinne reminded her.

"Pfft. He obviously had it in him to be one." Miranda paused and tapped her pencil on the table's surface, feeling an unexpected pang of hurt at the memory of Marshall's infidelity. Logical or not, that pained her more than his criminal acts. "But I can tell you for a fact that the gossip sheets got it wrong. He did not go looking for sex elsewhere because he wasn't getting any at home."

"You're preaching to the gossip-loathing choir here," Corinne said, setting the finished arrangement in the refrigerated storage case for a late-afternoon delivery. "I know firsthand how much garbage gets printed as truth. Then again, in Brenna's case, a lot of the garbage *is* the truth."

Corinne had been working at the flower shop for five years now, ever since Miranda had moved back to the small Rocky Mountain town where she'd grown up, and bought the business from its retiring owners.

She and Corinne had been good friends long enough for Miranda to know the extent of the conjecture printed about her employee's daughter, as well as the grief Brenna Sparks—the very same Ravyn Black mentioned in the Max Savage news segment—had caused Corinne. It was enough grief to bring about mother and daughter's current alienation.

But since the television mention gave Miranda the opening, she took advantage and voiced what had been on her mind. "I'd been wondering when the congressman's divorce was going to be final."

"Such a proud moment, too," Corinne said with a snort, "having to face that your daughter lacks the decency to keep her hands off a married man."

And now Teddy Eagleton wasn't married. Miranda sighed. "Ravyn—Brenna's an adult. She's been on her own for a long time now. And she's the one who'll have to answer for the things she's done."

"Really? Because she hasn't had to answer for much of anything yet." Corinne returned to her end of the worktable and flipped through the rest of the sale tickets to make certain she'd completed the day's most pressing orders. "And, unlike your ex, I wonder if she ever will."

Miranda knew Corinne was talking about the money she'd sent her daughter for college expenses—four years' worth of lab fees, textbooks, tuition for extra classes when Brenna had pretended to change her majors, as well as room and board. The money had been spent instead on funding her band.

Brenna had paid for equipment and instruments, a practice room, stage clothes and traveling, not even completing her first semester, and making Corinne feel like a fool—especially since Brenna had bribed her little sister Zoe to intercept mail sent by the university in Washington State in order to keep their mother from discovering the truth.

Miranda knew, too, that several times over the past six years—since Evermore's first album had hit it big—Brenna had tried to pay back her mother the money she'd stolen, and that Corinne had refused it, wanting nothing to do with what she called her daughter's ill-gotten gains.

It wasn't hard for Miranda to understand Corinne's feelings…except that it was. Brenna's "unexpected needs" had depleted the girls' college fund, and Corinne was now struggling to find what Zoe would require for the basics as a freshman next year. She was struggling, too, with trusting Zoe, who'd been just as culpable as Brenna.

"Will you have to testify at the retrial?"

Corinne's question snapped Miranda out of her reverie and dropped her back into the pit of worry she'd been doing a fairly good job of steering clear of. "I don't know. My attorney says there's a good chance I will, but he's doing all he can to keep it from happening. Trust me, if I have to fly into Baltimore, I'm going to fly out as fast as I can."

"You know, I'm surprised there haven't been more reporters snooping around, seeing how this *is* your family's home."

"You and me both." Not that they'd have an easy time finding her; when she'd returned to Mistletoe, she'd legally taken her mother's maiden name for her own—a protective measure she'd felt necessary at the time.

Corinne went on. "I figured the ones hungry enough for a statement would at least make the effort. Especially considering the scope of your ex's crimes."

A scope that had cost thousands of EMG employees their pensions and almost as many investors everything they'd owned. "Marshall was always a big believer in the grand scale. The more money, the more power, the more covers on *Forbes* the better."

"Or at least he *was* a big believer until he was sentenced to all those big years. I guess that was one grand scale he never saw coming." Corinne tore her copy of the next ticket from the order book and turned to study the shelf of vases, choosing an elegantly flared one of cut crystal. "You think the outcome will be any different this time?"

Miranda turned back to her laptop. Like her employee, she had work to do. "As far as him being guilty or innocent? No. But it better be different in that this time it sticks. I don't want to look up every five years to find a reporter sticking a microphone and camera in my face."

# 1
_____

*November...*

IT WASN'T IN Caleb McGregor's bag of reporter's tricks to go after a story by drinking himself under anyone's table, but here he was, at the Inn at Snow Falls' Club Crimson, in the lovers' resort of Mistletoe, Colorado, looking for clarity in the bottom of a glass.

Several glasses actually.

He knew better. Of course he knew better. But knowing better hadn't kept him from recently making the biggest mistake of his life. Neither did it negate the fact that he'd found many an answer to an intriguing question when his nose—or his blood alcohol level—was where it didn't belong.

Even when he was sober, his intuition rivaled that of the female population of Baltimore—the city he called his base of operations rather than home, *home* being a word with too much emotional resonance and Caleb not being a feelings kind of guy.

And that sixth sense had shifted into high gear the minute the lounge singer had taken the stage.

Unfortunately, the Scotch he'd downed had left him with a slippery grip on the instincts insisting he was sitting on top of a big fat scoop—one that might be as big and as fat as the exclusive he'd come here at Ravyn Black's invitation to get.

Whether or not that was the case, one thing was certain.

Club Crimson lived up to its vivid name.

The Inn at Snow Falls' nightclub was a kaleidoscope of reds, from the carpet splashed with sherry, claret and port-wine hues, to the padded bar and stools of scarlet, to the plush sofas and matching wing chairs in patterns of ruby and rose.

The decorative color scheme was not what Caleb found objectionable. After all, he'd yet to meet an Italian or Chinese restaurant he didn't like. Hell, his favorite baseball team had red in its name and wore the color proudly when taking the field at Fenway.

But when the design of a club was calculated to evoke a romantic, sexy mood, and that evocation lacked even a hint of the subtle finesse that made sexy *sexy,* and the entire set-up was set up in a town called Mistletoe, well…

Never let it be said that Caleb McGregor didn't embrace his cynicism wholeheartedly.

And then, as if the ornamental bloodbath wasn't enough, Club Crimson had gone so over the top in their efforts to promote romance as to hire a red-haired chanteuse and call her Candy Cane.

A textbook case of adding insult to injury. Or it would've been had she not manipulated the schmaltzy

lyrics into telling a story with the skill of Scheherazade—
and done so with a husky R & B style, and in a voice he
swore he'd heard before but couldn't for the drunken life
of him place.

He was falling for it all—the words that seduced him, the
costume that tempted him, the act as a whole that had him
mentally panting like a randy teen. Or a full-grown man with
more alcohol than reasoning skills at his disposal.

Considering the number of drinks he'd downed, the only
part of this that came as a surprise was the fact that he was
able to recognize the folly of his ways.

At least he'd had the good sense at the beginning of the
evening to claim a back corner booth. He was out of the way,
and in the perfect position to watch. And watch he did,
closely, enjoying himself more than was wise.

She was a looker, Ms. Cane, though considering the pretense of the rest of this place, he doubted her assets were
genuine. That didn't stop him from having a good time ogling
the plunging front of her cherry-colored gown.

He wasn't sure how women did it—kept their tits from
falling out of flesh-baring tops cut from their throats to their
navels. Some, he knew, had little to fear, but not in this case.
Whether Mother Nature or manufactured, she had a lot.

She was curvy, too, her cinched-in waist flaring into real hips
instead of not flaring at all. He liked hips. He liked a woman
with an ass. If he ran the world, women would be required by
law to be more than a pair of breasts on an androgynous body.

He'd amend the Constitution if he had to, put a picture of
Candy Cane next to one of Ravyn Black, the practically her-
maphroditic singer for the emo band Evermore he'd come
to Mistletoe to see, to illustrate the difference between ass
and no ass.

Yeah, that would be the perfect way to make his point. His point being…did he have a point?

Had he ever had a point? Was that the point his crossed eyes were seeing at the end of his nose? Or had his point become all soft and squishy and not pointy at all when he'd upended his glass and swallowed the last of his drink?

O…kay.

It was quitting time, heading-to-bed time. Time to just say no.

Or it would be if he wasn't stuck.

The pianist was playing the introductory notes to the singer's final song, and the crowd that had quieted when she walked onstage, that had done no more than whisper as she sang Frank Sinatra and Ella Fitzgerald and Harry Connick, Jr., had grown deathly still, pin-droppingly silent.

If Caleb got up now, he was likely to be shot.

Candy pulled the microphone from the stand she'd made love to during her previous song, and began to croon the opening lines of her last. Her hips swaying, she crossed the small corner stage and descended the steps into the mesmerized crowd drunk on whiskey, wine and love.

Her hair that he was sure was a wig—long, wavy, strawberry-blond—picked up and reflected the flashes of red thrown by the spinning disco ball, as did the sequins in the dress molded to her curves. So molded, in fact, that if it weren't for the peekaboo slit running up one thigh, he doubted she'd be able to walk.

He watched her wind her way through the gathered listeners, smiling, fingering one man's tie, brushing another's hair from his forehead, cupping a shoulder or stroking her finger along a forearm of their female companions. An equal-opportunity seductress, Caleb mused, finding his eyelids drifting lazily as he, too, fell prey to her spell.

A siren, she moved from table to table, the sultry sweep of her lashes, the alluring touch of her tongue to her lips, making men's knees weak, their palms sweaty, their blood run hot, the front of their pants—once flat against their abdomens—rise like pitched tents. He knew that's what was happening around the room because it was happening to him.

It didn't matter that he was the only person in the room sitting by himself. His reaction would've been the same had he been in the company of his mother, a date or a priest. He wasn't hard because he was alone, or because he was lonely. He was hard because Candy Cane had made him that way.

But the fact that this was a group erection cheapened what he felt—or so he tried to convince himself, since he didn't want to feel anything.

And then something else happened. She turned just so, moved to the perfect spot, leaned against the back of a sofa at the ideal angle with the lights exactly right. The moment didn't last longer than a blink before it was gone, and she'd bowed her body toward another sap in the crowd.

But it stuck with him, wouldn't let him go, and he studied her instead of looking away, stared at her instead of chalking up what he thought he was seeing to too much Scotch on a stomach empty of anything else.

What he thought he was seeing was a familiar face. A familiar face to go with the voice he could've sworn he recognized at the beginning of her set. A recognition he'd then dismissed because of how many times the server had replaced the single malt in his snifter.

Now he really did need a drink, and he needed it to be hot, black and fully caffeinated so he could make sense of the psychedelic swirls and splatters of reds Club Crimson had painted in his mind.

His job depended on rumors. He listened, he verified, he discarded. He'd been doing it for ten years, writing a celebrity gossip column that had started out small and gone into national syndication twenty-four months after launch. It was so popular, it was featured during what one TV network called their "celebrity beat," and had its own Web site to boot.

Caleb McGregor was Max Savage, the notorious "Snoop with the Scoop," loved, lauded and feared far and wide by politicians, society players and celebrities alike for his sarcastic riffs on what his audience demanded and deemed newsworthy about those in the public eye.

Not that anyone at the inn knew who he was, or that he was here by invitation for an exclusive—the very private wedding of Ravyn Black and Teddy Eagleton. Over the next few days, he'd be covering the preparations leading up to the big event. But as always, he was posing as a member of Max Savage's street team. Not even Ravyn knew he was Max.

The only people who knew his identity, who would ever know or have need to, were his agent, his attorney and his editor. When he'd set off down tabloid road ten years ago, he'd made sure his only connection was to the Max Savage machine, not to the alter ego itself.

It was a decision that had turned out to be a sanity-saver, keeping his personal business out of the limelight. And it was going to make it a whole lot easier to transition to life after Max—a retirement that would have him hanging up his gear as soon as he finished this gig.

Yes, he found the energy of chasing down nonstop leads more intoxicating than the boredom of waiting for a big story to break. But he'd never thought he'd end up stooping to the level he had, reporting on celebutantes flashing their bare crotches or finding fame through night-vision sex tapes.

Neither had he thought himself capable of betraying a confidence, so wrapped up in the thrill that he hadn't realized he'd gone too far until it was too late. Until he'd ruined a career by telling the truth. Until he'd lost a lifelong friend because he'd been drunk on the rush of the scoop.

He'd give anything to take back the last month, to think before revealing what his best friend Del, a music star in his own right, had shared in confidence about his Christian pop star fiancée's drug problem…but life didn't work that way.

Caleb couldn't change what he'd done, but he could damn well make sure it never happened again. Right now, however, it was vital that he get his act together. Candy had finished her tour of the rest of the club and was making her way toward him.

Drinking alone and slumped in his seat made him an easy target. Being male made him vulnerable—even knowing her act was a ruse. Last he'd checked, knowledge didn't necessarily work as an inoculant. Especially with his susceptibility to her charms camped out in his pants.

Except for her spotlight, the bar light and the patterns of color thrown off by the disco ball's spin, the club was dark. His corner was even darker, giving him the privacy he needed to adjust his crotch before she reached him.

And then she was there, singing to him, seducing him, the pull in her gaze mesmerizing as she perched her hip against the edge of his table and stretched, draping herself toward him strategically as if she'd done this hundreds of times for hundreds of other men.

Her neckline plunged to tease him. The slope of her shoulder as she leaned close, the movement of her neck, chin and mouth as she sang, teased him more. But what teased him most of all was knowing he should know her, being unable to place her, and sitting here too inebriated to do anything to find out.

He told himself to remember everything about her, to store the sound of her voice in the memory banks he could access most quickly when his wits returned. He didn't hold out much hope for success. She had him stupid, bewitched.

Fluidly, the redheaded chanteuse rolled herself up and off the table, pivoting with an elegance that left him breathless—and therefore, thankfully, unable to groan and give himself away—as she slid to sit in his lap.

It wasn't his lap as much as one leg, but the move put the swell of her bottom against the swell of his fly, and he could only hope the part of him making intimate contact with her wasn't as apparent to her as he feared.

She seemed comfortable, in her element, looping her arm around his neck, looking into his eyes, drawing the song to a close with a breathy, bluesy, brush of words against his cheek as the pianist wrapped up his accompaniment, holding the final notes.

That was when the applause began.

And that was when she kissed him.

He hadn't seen it coming.

He knew the soft teasing press of her mouth to his was part of the act, but he hadn't expected it, and he wasn't thinking straight, and he was running way low on resistance, so he did what any healthy red-blooded male would do with a healthy red-blooded female wanting to lock lips.

He kissed her back.

He caught her off guard. She was bargaining on compliance, thinking he would accept her doing her thing without interfering, interrupting or doing his back. But Caleb wasn't cut from a compliant cloth. And kissing Candy Cane was fun. Or it was until he realized he was the one who was stirred.

Lips on lips was one thing, but this was more. Way more,

and his blood heated and rushed. He opened his mouth to taste her. She gave in, letting his tongue inside to flirt and slick over hers.

He had a vague sense of people around them clapping and whistling, cheering them on, of the pianist's fingers lingering over his instrument's keys, drawing out the moment that had already gone on too long.

But mostly he was aware of Candy's scent like a field of sweet flowers around him, and the touch of her fingers against his nape, the tiny massaging circles she made there too personal for a public display.

He had to let her go before things got any further out of hand, he realized, realizing, too, that he had sobered. He pulled his mouth away and tilted his head back to get the best look that he could into her eyes.

He saw her surprise, then her fear. The first he'd anticipated; he'd felt it himself. The second emotion set the pump on his snoop-and-scoop machine to maximum. Fear? What the hell did she have to be afraid of?

"Who are you?" he asked as she got to her feet, the smile she gave him reaching no farther than her mouth and as much for the crowd as for him.

"I'm the woman you'll never forget," she told him, blowing him a parting kiss before returning to the stage.

Once there, she took her final bow with a flourish, gave props to the pianist then vanished behind the curtain that came down to swallow the stage.

She had it right. He wouldn't forget. But what she had no way of knowing was that, impending retirement or not, big-time screwup or not, he planned to dig up a whole lot more stuff to remember. Stuff he was pretty damn sure Ms. Candy Cane didn't want anyone to find out.

# 2

WELL. That had been interesting, Miranda Kelly mused ruefully, standing in her dressing room, staring at her reflection and finding Candy Cane staring back.

She had yet to remove her costume—a costume that was more than the dress or the shoes or the colored contacts or the wig. The whole persona of Candy was everything she wasn't.

As Miranda, she wore glasses, though she did accessorize with fashionable frames to emphasize the green of her eyes. Her own hair was auburn in contrast to Candy's strawberry-blond, and cropped close in a wispy elfin cut.

Her skin was nowhere as smooth as Candy's, plus it was ridiculously freckled—a fact that she'd hidden from Baltimore society when she'd lived there behind a cool façade of flawlessly made-up skin, French twists and perfect posture, the veneer of a high-profile life.

She was nothing if not a chameleon.

But, wow. Kissing an audience member? Had she really been so stupidly careless? She'd told Corinne several months ago that her biggest fear about testifying at Marshall's retrial was suffering a repeat of the media madness and losing her sanctuary in Mistletoe as a result. It was imperative that she draw no attention to herself to keep that from happening.

Oh, sure, she flirted and toyed with and played with and teased members of the crowd every night, but she did so as Candy; Miranda was off-limits to the visitors at the inn. That personal touch was part of Candy's act and the only outlet Miranda had to keep her feminine wiles from rusting.

She hadn't dated at all in the five years she'd been here, and hadn't enjoyed more than conversation with the male company she regularly kept. Mistletoe, Colorado, was not a hotbed of sexy, intelligent, available men.

It was a lovers' resort, a place where the people listening to her sing would not be focused on her but on their partners. And that was exactly as it should be. Her rumination was not at all a complaint. Her complaint was that *she* had behaved so rashly, so…thoughtlessly. With Marshall once again in the news, she couldn't afford to stand out, to be noticed.

So who was he, the man she had kissed, the man who had let her, who had kissed her back with a mouth that tasted like aged Scotch and heat? And what was he doing alone in a town that catered to lovers—most of whom had sought out the hideaway specifically because of the privacy it afforded?

She sank onto her vanity bench, still shocked. She could not believe how impressively she had screwed up.

No one passed through Mistletoe by chance, or planned a night out at Club Crimson unless they were staying at the Inn at Snow Falls. The town was off the beaten path, the inn stuck in its own time warp. Visitors were here for a reason.

That meant the likelihood she would see *him* again was spectacular. And with this combustible thing between them having flared in such a sparkling display, her odds of screwing up again were even higher. She couldn't let that happen—not with the publicity from Marshall's trial looming.

Before the career move a decade ago that had taken her

from Denver to Baltimore, and before meeting Marshall and marrying him in the same church where she sang in the choir, she'd spent all but her college years in Mistletoe, growing up an only child of parents who worked in the school district here.

When her life as Mrs. Gordon had soured—not a surprising development considering her husband's indictment for fraud and the dredging up of his affairs during his trial, she'd found herself thinking back to the simple, uncluttered magic of this place she still thought of as home.

In Mistletoe, discretion was paramount. It was even more so at the Inn at Snow Falls. The resort's staff was merciless in vetting credentials, checking IDs and keeping out media riffraff.

She'd seen them in action, and knew that facet of the hideaway's reputation was what brought celebrities and public figures here for intimate trysts, photos of which they didn't want splashed across tabloid covers.

That was the atmosphere she, too, had needed, and with the help of trusted friends, she had escaped the East Coast, leaving the gossips floundering.

For months after, newsmen who followed society scandals had hunted her, wanting the exclusive of her exile. She'd watched from the safety of her snowy cocoon and experienced a flurry of emotions, her feelings ultimately boiling down to one.

She hated the press. H-a-t-e-d reporters and their supposed journalistic integrity. They were vultures. They'd treated her like carrion during Marshall's trial and the divorce. They were as responsible as her ex for making her life hell. But no more.

She refused to spend another moment feeling bared and naked, flayed, exposed to her bones like an instructional cadaver or a plasticized body in a museum display. That's how it had seemed, having the population of the northern Atlantic states knowing minute details of her life....

Her propensity for speeding through traffic lights. How she spent more time on her own charity work than socializing with Marshall or at home. The way an hour of Ashtanga yoga left her smelling as though she hadn't bathed in days. Whether her salon's beauty technician gave her a bikini wax or a Brazilian. And if any of those things sent Marshall into the arms—and beds—of all those other women.

Despite her very public night job she now held, no one had found her, partly because of the disguise she wore onstage—and that was one of the reasons she wore it, to limit any obvious connection between her two selves—and partly because of how well the residents of Mistletoe protected their own.

But the main reason her cover hadn't been blown—besides her legal change of name—was that the only outsiders she mixed with were the customers who came in to order plants and floral arrangements from Under the Mistletoe.

Or such had been the case until she'd fallen all over the gorgeous stranger who'd kissed her until she felt as though she was going to die.

Smart. Real smart. A veritable genius of a cookie.

She dropped her forehead to the vanity's surface and groaned—which only made things worse because it brought to mind all the things he'd made her feel. She'd forgotten how sweet it could be to slide her tongue against a man's seeking to enter her mouth.

Such an exquisite pleasure, that first sweet connection, its wetness, its promise, its warmth. She'd enjoyed a comfortable sex life with Marshall—until he'd begun finding his comfort elsewhere—but she never had seen stars.

She could get used to stars, she told herself, sitting up to study her reflection. She didn't know what she was looking for, something different or new, a visible indication that something within her had changed because of a starry kiss.

She knew that nothing had, that nothing could have. She'd been on her stranger's table and in his lap no more than seconds, and her mouth had been pressed to his, seeking, searching, aching, almost no time at all.

The only thing to change had been her perfect record at staying smart. Five years sober, and she'd fallen off the wagon because of a man. Stupid, stupid, stupid. If her actions became a time bomb and blew up in her face, she would have no one to blame but herself.

"Argh," she roared, surging up off the bench. She needed someone to talk to. Reassurance that she hadn't screwed herself. A reinforcing slap to the head telling her that everything she wanted was *not* in a stranger's kiss—no matter that it had felt as if that was exactly where she would find it.

# 3

"Do you believe in love at first sight?"

Alan Price, Club Crimson's manager and overflow bartender, stared at Miranda as if she'd grown two heads, which she supposed was about the size of it. She had her Miranda head, and her Candy head, and Alan was one of the few people who knew both well, working with her here at the club, and having lived next door to her when they were kids.

"Was it love at first sight with me and Patrice?" he asked, clipboard in hand while he did his nightly inventory, a shock of his sun-bleached hair falling forward to hide his frown. "Is that what you're asking?"

Miranda settled more comfortably onto the bar stool in the now-empty lounge, leaning an elbow on the bar and propping her chin in her hand. "Tell me about meeting Patrice. I'm in the mood for a good love story."

Alan had calmed her down with a couple of drinks when she'd blasted into the club after her dressing-room panic attack, promising her the crowd had thought nothing of the spice she'd added to her show.

He'd calmed her enough, in fact, that she was almost ready to call it a night, to head back to her dressing room, to strip off Candy…and then hope her ancient import started when she went out in the cold to go home. One of these days, she really did need to spring for a new car.

A reformed ski bum, having shed the *bum* part for respectability, Alan shook his head as if too busy cleaning up to humor her. "You know how I met Patrice. I've heard her tell you the story more than once."

Feeling all fluid and relaxed, Miranda sighed. "She's told me, yes. I want to hear it from you."

He took away her wineglass, added it to the crate of dirties destined for the kitchen before he left for the night. After that, he pointed at the clock on the wall at the end of the bar. The hands, shaped like corkscrews, were edging toward 1:00 a.m., the club having closed at midnight.

He yawned for emphasis. "She's waiting for me to get home. If she calls, I'm handing the phone to you."

"And I'll tell her it's your fault, not mine," Miranda said before sticking out her tongue, the back and forth a familiar pattern from their years as friends.

"How the hell in any universe is it my fault?"

"You could be halfway through the story by now, for all that you're dawdling." Men. Why was it so hard for them to talk about their emotional investments? They certainly had no trouble talking about their portfolios. It wasn't like she'd asked him to open a vein and bleed out his feelings for Patrice all over the bar.

Then again, maybe it wasn't copping to love at first sight he was dodging. Maybe it was the embarrassment of not having been on his game when they met, she mused, smiling to herself as she recalled the story Patrice had shared.

"I was skiing," he told her, obviously taking note of the look on her face and scowling as he wiped a rag over the bar, his motions so furious that she thought he'd rub away the finish. "I crashed, broke my leg. Patrice was on the patrol team that rescued me."

The short, to-the-point, testosterone version. She wanted

more. She wanted all the heat and the want and the feelings. "What about the eye contact? The jolt to your heart? The tingle you felt when she pulled off her gloves and laid the backs of her fingers against your cheek?"

"That was frostbite."

Miranda laughed, the sound echoing loudly in the quiet room. "You, Alan Price, are so full of crap. You felt it all just like Patrice did, and you know it."

He stopped scrubbing the already clean bar, and gave her a look, color high on his sharp cheekbones. "Then you didn't need to hear it from me, did you?"

"Sure I did. You've restored my faith that men will be men, and nothing there will ever change." He'd also reminded her that she wasn't missing out by being alone, no matter how magic a man's kiss. "Just the facts. No embellishments. No personalization. No deeper meaning."

His expression was very male and almost angry. "We feel things, Miranda. We may not talk about them, but they're there."

Well. That shut her up. She reached for his hand. "I'm sorry. I'm tired, and tonight threw me off-kilter. I guess I'm the one looking for deeper meaning, though I'm not sure why. Maybe I just need an explanation for what I did."

"And I told you. Candy hit a hell of a groove, that's all. The audience enjoyed it. There isn't any deeper meaning, so stop wasting time trying to find it."

Easy for him to say. He wasn't the one whose lips still felt the kiss, whose pulse had yet to quit racing. She toyed with the seam in the bar's padded edge, picking at threads that weren't there. "Let's hope it was a one-time thing. With Marshall's retrial coming up, Miranda can't afford for Candy to start getting careless."

"Does that mean you haven't changed your mind about singing at the Christmas dance?"

"No. I haven't." She wouldn't take Candy Cane out of Club Crimson, even as a favor to Patrice. She'd reiterated to Alan and his wife all the reasons why when first asked to perform at the Mistletoe County High dance.

"The kids would love it," Alan said, wooing her by wiggling both brows. "All they know is the legend of the sexy redhead who sings at the inn."

And if Miranda had her way, that was all the students would ever know about her. "The kids would *not* love it. I'm an old fart who sings old-fart songs. If anyone needs to perform for them, it's Zoe."

Corinne's younger daughter was seventeen and as brilliant a singer as her sister. Her voice was a deep, throaty alto, incredibly rich and mature for a girl so young.

Zoe was the reason Miranda had used a chunk of her obscenely large divorce settlement to establish the Candy Cane Scholarship for the Arts, and why she continued to funnel into it all the money she made at the club.

Even if Corinne had her reasons for not accepting Brenna's offer to repay the misappropriated funds plus interest, Zoe was too good to be hidden away. A legitimate study of voice and music seemed to Miranda the perfect compromise. The scholarship was her way of putting her money where her mouth was.

Miranda looked back at Alan. "I wish Patrice would add her to the program. Zoe could use the exposure."

"She's going to," Alan said, thrilling Miranda to bits. "But the kids know Zoe. Patrice was hoping for a big-name headliner."

"I heard her sister's in town," Miranda said, thinking about

Corinne and her relationships with her girls. Sooner or later mother needed to meet older daughter halfway—even if only for the sake of the younger. "Patrice should try to snag Ravyn."

"That might work if Patrice were willing to forget everything Mistletoe stands for and invade Ravyn's privacy, which she's not going to do. And if Brenna and Corinne weren't on the outs. There's no way Patrice is going behind Corinne's back just to make points with the kids."

Miranda knew he was right. As cool a coup as it would be for the senior class to have Evermore's lead singer at their Christmas dance, there were a whole lot of circumstances in the way of it happening.

Besides, with Ravyn—Brenna—estranged from her family, her visit to Mistletoe sans the band pretty much confirmed the rumors of her romantic liaison with right-wing and conveniently newly single congressman Teddy Eagleton, who Miranda had seen in the lobby earlier in the day.

Whatever the two were doing here, mentioning it to Corinne was nothing Miranda wanted to do. Especially since the other woman might soon be dealing with the reporters turned away by security from the inn. Having experienced the same, Miranda had great sympathy for what Corinne had ahead of her.

"You finished with that?" Alan asked, looking over Miranda's head.

She started to tell him that he'd already done his conscientious-bartender-and-childhood-friend duty and taken her wineglass away. Then he realized she wasn't the one to whom he was speaking.

She glanced over her shoulder and peered into the dark. A man was walking toward them from the club's far corner, a coffee cup and saucer in hand.

He was tall, and he rolled with a swagger, his legs long, his hips and waist narrow, his shoulders wide beneath the dark jacket he wore with his jeans…his jeans…

She'd sat in the lap of a man wearing jeans, a man who'd watched her show from the club's far corner. *Crap and double crap*. She turned back quickly, hissing at her ex-friend to get his attention.

"He's been here all this time and you didn't tell me?" Dear God, had she given herself away? Had he overheard Alan call her Miranda? Had she confessed that she was still reeling from the contact of their lips and their tongues? "What the hell is wrong with you?"

Alan smirked his ex-friend enjoyment of her distress. "Patrice said you've been extra moody lately. I figured you might need to get laid."

"I hate you, you know."

"I know. I hate you, too."

Thank God she hadn't taken off her wig. That was the only thought that crossed her mind before the stranger who kissed like a god climbed onto the stool beside her, filling the space as if it had been waiting a lifetime for him to find it. Uh, yeah. This couldn't be good.

"Thanks for the coffee," he told Alan, giving Miranda his profile to study as he handed the cup and saucer across the bar. "I wasn't sure I'd be able to make it to my room, or even remember where I put it."

As hard as she tried not to, Miranda couldn't help a soft laugh; the sound had him swiveling slowly toward her, cocking his head, drinking her in until she forgot to breathe and changed her mind about this being good.

"Laugh at me, laugh with me. I'll take either one."

Oh, he was sharp. And gorgeous. Somehow she'd missed

the full extent of his gorgeousness when she'd been in his lap, but there was still nothing she wouldn't give right now for a big fat hole in the ground.

A hole swallowing her would keep her from looking at his mouth. His mouth, his lips, his tongue, his teeth. She remembered them all. She wanted them all. She wanted more.

She wanted him. She'd been right the first time. This was not good.

"Caleb McGregor," he said, offering her his hand.

After a moment, she took it. "Candy Cane."

"According to the marquee," he said, before letting her go.

Touché, she thought, refusing to confirm his assumption with body language or voice. "I'm not sure if I should thank you or beg your forgiveness."

The mouth that had been all over hers and made her into a marshmallow smiled. "There's nothing to forgive, and I'm pretty sure I'm the one who should be thanking you."

He was smart. Smooth. Cutely self-deprecating rather than smarmy. Or maybe that was the kiss talking, and she should be listening to her survival instincts instead. "You were a good sport, and I'm sorry if I embarrassed you. I don't usually get that…personal with the audience."

He paused a moment, taking her in. "Then I'm glad I was there when you decided to change things up."

*Spice,* Alan had called it. Adding spice to Candy's routine. If only it were that simple, adding, changing, but the truth rarely was. And this particular truth wasn't easy to admit.

There had been no conscious decision in what she'd done. Her brain had had nothing to do with her sliding into his lap. Hormones and lust were responsible for her pressing her mouth to his and giving him her tongue. She'd seen him. She'd wanted him. She'd taken him.

And now here he was, sitting beside her, close, his knee brushing her thigh when he swiveled on the stool, a whiff of Scotch and coffee reaching her nose along with the scent of something earthy and warm.

She needed to excuse herself. To go. She was in so much trouble here. So, of course, she went ahead and made it worse. "What brings you to Mistletoe, Caleb? You're not here alone, are you?"

"Actually, I am," he said, bursting that insulating bubble.

Kiss or no kiss, his having a companion would've put him off-limits. Now he wasn't, which was going to make it hard to say no—to him, to herself…especially with Alan's comment about her needing to get laid echoing with more veracity than she liked.

She pushed aside the noise of that echo, focusing on Caleb's hand that rested flat on the bar. His fingers were long, thick, the backs broad and dusted with golden hair. She closed her eyes, opened them slowly, hoped he couldn't read her mind because, oh, there were so many places she wanted his touch.

"Alone? Really?" She cleared her throat. "I'm surprised."

He glanced over, arching a brow, questioning, curious. "Surely you get the occasional single up here."

She stared at him, studied him, liked too much what she was seeing…his stylishly mussed hair, a warm brown toasted with highlights…his eyes that were a gorgeous blend of gold and bronze…his mouth that she was certain did more things than kiss well.

Good. Not good. She didn't know the difference anymore. "I don't mingle enough with the guests to be sure, but I can't say I've seen anyone not part of a couple."

"Well, now you have," he told her, teased her. "Seen someone who's not, and mingled."

She looked down, went back to picking at the bar. "I'm just breaking all sorts of rules tonight."

"Must be the company you're keeping."

"I can't think of any other reason." It was hard to think of anything with her heart in her throat, choking her, cutting off her ability to breathe.

He watched her hands, then looked up, his eyes saying more than his words, saying that he knew what she was feeling, the extreme pull she was fighting. That he was fighting the same. "Can you think of one that would keep us from getting a drink?"

She nodded. "The bar's closed."

"That's a hard one to get around," he said, adding, "though I can think of one solution."

"No," she told him. Absolutely not. "I won't come up to your room for a nightcap."

"Rules?"

"Rules," she said, and nodded again.

"Too bad about the rules," he said, and she laughed. And then she stopped because he leaned close to say, "You're a hell of a kisser."

Well. She'd been hoping to hear him tell her goodbye. Or hear that he wasn't much for obeying the rules. He seemed the sort, a bit brash, a bit dangerous. He'd obviously convinced Alan to let him hang out long after closing.

"It was all part of the act," was what she finally said, ignoring the flutter of her pulse as he breathed her in and sighed, and the tongue of flame in her belly when he came back with, "The hell it was," a response that begged the question, *Where do we go from here?*

Alan clearing his throat pushed her to answer. "If you can stomach the mess, I have a bottle of Drambuie in my dressing room."

He didn't respond right away, looking her over, staring into her eyes. His were hard to read in this light, but that didn't lessen the impact of his gaze, or the heat simmering in the air around them.

She wasn't sure if she should take back the offer, if she'd been too forward in making it. If he had wanted nothing from her. Or had just wanted an acknowledgment that the kiss had been way out of line.

That wasn't how she'd read him, but she was so out of practice with men—

"A man in your dressing room. That's not against the rules?"

"I don't know," she said, sliding from her stool, unable to stop herself from giving in to this very big wrong that had her nape tingling, other places doing the same. "You're the first one I've ever invited to join me."

# 4

CALEB COULDN'T BELIEVE his good fortune. First, that the bartender had told him to take his time with the coffee. Second, that Candy Cane had so easily fallen prey to his charms.

Especially when he had so few.

If what he did have qualified as charming at all.

Not many people thought so.

As she'd gestured in the direction of her dressing room and turned for him to follow, he'd watched the subtle exchange that had passed between the redheaded siren and the bartender.

The man who'd served Caleb the coffee he'd so desperately needed hadn't seemed insulted or injured that she'd invited him back for a drink. Neither had he gone into protective, big-brother, hurt-her-and-I'll-kick-your-ass mode.

So far, so good.

Having witnessed the conversation the two had shared earlier, Caleb assumed the bartender and Candy were good friends. Not that he'd heard any of what they'd said, but he had noticed the casual nature of their exchange and the comfortable intimacy between them.

All that was to say…either the man behind the bar with the ski-bum look knew Candy could take care of herself, or knew Caleb was the one heading into trouble. Judging by the sway of her hips as she walked through the club and his body's primal reaction, Caleb heading into trouble was true either way.

He told himself to look up, to look away, over her shoulders, above her head, down at the floor. But her hips had been in his lap at the same time her tongue had been in his mouth, and that was all he could think about. That, and wanting more.

Or so it was until he reminded himself of why he was here, why he'd wanted the coffee in the first place. The recognition he'd needed to be sober enough to place. Yes, he was getting out of the biz, but he couldn't give up his curiosity any more than he could cut off a leg. If he figured her out and found her story worth telling, well…he'd cross the bridge of what to do when he got to it.

She led him through the bar, across the stage and to a door down the hallway behind the wings.

There was no name, no star, nothing to indicate where they were. It could just as easily have been a broom closet for the lack of signage. But she opened the door, and like a beast in rut, he followed her in.

"Like I said," she reminded him as she flipped on the lights. "A mess."

It didn't look any worse than his place, he mused, walking inside as she shut the door behind him. The floor was covered with the same red carpeting as the rest of the club. The walls were painted off-white with a pink tinge —or else the semi-gloss was reflecting the floor.

A closet with a six-foot rod took up the wall opposite one with six feet worth of mirrors. The accordion doors were open, showing red tops and bottoms on and off hangers, dresses draped over the pole, other items of clothing puddled on the floor and covering dozens of shoes flung here and there.

He turned toward the mirror, and she pushed in behind him, closing the doors as if to hide her shame. He wondered if her house was in the same disarray, and how she could look so put together when she dressed in a danger zone.

"I promise, I'm much neater than this in the rest of my life. For some reason when I'm here, I tend to let down my hair— as it were," she tacked on, nodding to a shelf of wigs he hadn't yet noticed.

"You didn't fool me for a minute," he told her, reaching for the strawberry strands where they caressed her bare shoulder. He allowed his fingers to linger on her skin, her soft skin that in this light was obviously freckled, leaving them there, tempting himself. Testing himself.

She was warm, smooth, and he couldn't help but think about the rest of her that was still covered, wondering how soft she'd be elsewhere, thinking, too, about her mouth and the touch of her tongue to his, wanting that again, wanting her taste, wanting another jolt of that unexpected heat.

It took her several seconds to move, and his gut tightened while he waited. He watched her face as it broadcast the push-pull conflict driving her, push winning out in the end and demanding distance and space between them—though pull sizzled in the air that had grown sharp with expectation.

She opened one of the lockerlike cabinets stacked next to the closet doors. "I have a bottle," she said, showing him the Drambuie and the single glass tumbler she had. "But I only have one glass."

He took it from her hand, took the bottle, too, uncapped it and poured. He drank, then offered the glass to her. "So we share."

She took it and sipped without hesitation. He closed up the bottle and set it on the vanity next to a pair of narrow-framed eyeglasses. A contact-lens case and a bottle of solution sat nearby, as did a brush with several strands of short dark hair caught in the bristles.

Caleb smiled, and turned back to the mysterious faux-redhead, thinking how much he'd like to see her in nothing but her freckles and her real hair. He swallowed hard, fighting the rush of blood through his veins, and asked, "What do singles do around here for fun?"

"Leave?" she suggested, and laughed softly, looking into the tumbler and avoiding looking at him. "The only place to get a drink besides Club Crimson is Manny's, but it's more a local watering hole. There's Fish and Cow Chips—"

"Seafood and steak?" he asked, cutting her off with a grimace at that mental image.

She held the glass close to her chest as she finally met his gaze. "Yes, it's very poorly named. Though the food is amazing."

"No theater with dinner?"

"Nope," she said, handing him their shared drink. "And if you want a movie, well, you drive down the mountain into Golden, or you get a satellite dish and be happy that you're only six months behind the pop-culture curve."

He wondered what she'd think if she knew he swung the bell for that curve. He leaned back against the edge of the vanity, swirled the herb-flavored liqueur in the glass, enjoyed the waft of aroma. Enjoyed even more being in close quarters with this woman he very much wanted to figure out.

"What do you do when you're not Candy?"

She gave him a teasing smile. "I'm always Candy."

"Then what does Candy do when she's not onstage?" he asked taking a step closer, feeling the crackle of electricity burning fiercely between them, a live-wire connection he swore he could reach out and touch.

This time she gave him a shake of her finger, a school-teacher scolding a pupil for his impertinence, with a wickedly sexy gleam in her eye. "Ah, that's something I only share with friends and family."

"Hmm. In a town this size, that must cover everyone." And then because he needed to know… "Including the man in your life?" Or the men who once were.

She shook her head, sat on one end of the vanity bench, took the glass when he offered it and allowed his fingers to linger against hers. "No lovers, current or ex. Not for a very long time."

"That's a shame." He joined her on the bench. The seat was only so long, and their thighs brushed. She stayed where she was. Even when he shifted to touch her hip, her arm, she didn't move. "You're a beautiful woman."

At the base of her throat, her pulse jumped, but that was her only response. She sat still, the glass of honeyed Scotch liqueur held between both of her hands in her lap. The walking slit in her skirt had parted to reveal the length of her stocking-covered thigh. The deep V-neck in her top high-lighted the inner swells of her breasts.

It was hard to keep his gaze on her face with all that bounty to feast on, but her face along with her voice would help him figure out if he knew her—though he had to admit he was quickly forgetting he'd ever had such a hunch. He was much more interested in exploring the rest of her, and doing so for very selfish reasons.

"You never did tell me why you were here," she finally said. A hitch in her chest when she breathed in revealed the state of her composure.

He liked that she reacted to him, that he wasn't the only one here caught up by anticipation and need. "I'm attending a wedding."

She gave a nod, a smile. "Another celebrity off the market?"

"It's a private gig, but, yeah. It'll be a pretty big deal when it makes the news." He raised a brow, raised the drink. "I'm sure you could snoop into what's going on, if you really wanted to know. A perk of working here and all."

That caused her chin to come up, a frown to crease her brow—a response he hadn't expected, and one he filed away. "I don't think so," she said. "People come here because they don't have to worry about being stalked or hounded by the media, or by the staff."

He made a mental note not to reveal the hounding he had done, the stalking, definitely not the betrayal. Reaching for their shared glass, he set it on the floor beneath the bench, then shifted to better face her before cupping his hand to her cheek. "I'm sorry. Offending you is the last thing I'd ever want to do."

"What's the first?" she asked, her lashes drifting down in a soft sexy sweep before she raised her gaze in invitation.

The heat he'd been feeling grew to engulf him, and the surface of his skin fairly burned. "Are you sure you want to know?"

She nodded, the look in her eyes one of hunger, of craving, one that caused him to ache. When he leaned toward her, he wasn't a journalist. He was only a man. A man who hadn't been able to stop thinking about her since melting into her kiss.

And so he kissed her again. This time he didn't have to be still or discreet. He was able to close his eyes and give in to the desire that rolled through him the moment their lips made contact.

He continued to hold her face as he slanted his mouth over hers and coaxed her to open. She turned toward him, leaned into him, allowed him the access he wanted, and met him with her tongue.

The kiss was tentative, a gentle exploration. He didn't want to rush her or push her or frighten her away. She didn't want to give in too quickly or show him too much of her need. He felt it, though, in the tense way she held her jaw, in the tautness of her neck as she kept her head straight.

She'd admitted to having no lover. He had a feeling it had also been a while since she'd had something as simple as a kiss. Not that this kiss was any simpler than the one in the club, any less arousing or potent.

The difference was in being alone and able to complicate things as thoroughly as they wanted, with no one to interrupt, with nothing to keep the kiss from becoming more.

She pushed forward, exhaled tiny moans into his mouth, used her teeth to nip, her tongue to bathe the damage, her lips to play catch and release with his.

Then she shifted her position, turning her body toward him instead of the vanity, and looped her arms around his neck, raking the fingers of one hand up his nape and into his hair. Her hunger was a match lit to his.

The hand with which he'd been cupping her face moved to cup her slender neck. His other hand found its way to the slit in her dress, and to her thigh. He slipped his fingers between her legs, and she parted them in invitation, whimpering as she did.

He stroked down to her knee, up to the seam where the sequined fabric split, but no farther. As much as he wanted to go there, he needed a sign that she was ready to take things that far.

She gave it to him with a softly whispered, "Please," and

with a hand that guided his higher between her legs. Before he'd even cupped the mound of her sex, he felt her moisture and her heat.

He used the edge of his index finger to play her, pressing it against her, rubbing it back and forth over her clit. She jumped, shuddered, blew short, sweet panting breaths against the edge of his open mouth.

"Good?" he asked.

"So good," she answered, the words more moaned than spoken. "Can you—"

"Make you come?"

"Yes. Oh, yes." This time the words rolled up from the back of her throat, a growled order as much as a plea.

He smiled, covered her mouth, bruised her with his kiss until his erection strained against his fly. When he pulled away, she urged him back.

But first… "Your hose—"

"Get rid of them."

He loved a woman who knew what she wanted. One brave enough not to let propriety get in the way. He found the seam between her legs, dug his fingers against it and tore the fabric free, finding a scrap of a thong covering her sex, and scooping it aside.

She was smooth and damp, and she gasped when he touched her. He moved his lips to the base of her neck and parted her folds with his finger. Her throat vibrated with the sounds she made as he toyed with her, sliding a finger inside her, flicking his thumb over her clit.

She tucked her chin to her chest, closing her eyes, gouging her fingers into his shoulders hard enough to leave marks, and rode his hand, pumping her hips where she sat, sliding on and off his finger.

He ran the flat of his tongue along her collarbone, kissed his way back to her throat, moved to the swell of her breast and pushed her dress aside. He found her nipple and sucked, penetrating her sex with a second finger, rolling the tip of her breast with his lips. She was close now.

He'd hit the right rhythm, found the right combination of pressure and motion, and he kept it up, stroking, rubbing, in and out and around. She tensed, grew wetter. Her breathing quickened, becoming labored and shallow and damp.

And then she cried out, tossing back her head as her orgasm consumed her. He watched the fierce sweep of emotions cross her face, felt her sex contract around him, found himself awash on an amazing high at being able to give this to her, share this with her. At pleasing her so completely.

She came down quickly, shaking, her hands sliding from his shoulders to his biceps, color rising to her cheeks as she dipped her head. "I can't believe—"

"Believe." He didn't want her to feel self-conscious, or awkward at what she'd allowed him to see. He wanted her to bask in the lingering sensation, not embarrassment.

"But you didn't. It's not right—"

He smiled, leaned forward to nuzzle the skin beneath her ear. "If you want to do something about that, I won't say no."

# 5

TEN MINUTES LATER Miranda and Caleb were sneaking into the Inn at Snow Falls' kitchen, ready to feed their hunger with leftovers since the lack of a condom had kept them from feeding it in more intimate ways.

Miranda was still smiling at Caleb's lack of preparedness. Her own lack was just as sad, but then she never expected to cross paths with eligible men. She'd resigned herself to a life of having sex with herself and her vibrators, and poured out her sensuality onstage.

But a sexy, gorgeous and extremely persuasive man like Caleb—for him not to have a condom at the ready for the women he must meet… She glanced back at him, her smile widening and taking over her face.

"Are you laughing at me or with me this time?" he asked from behind her as she waved at the dishwasher, Earnesto, who winked back a promise not to tattle to the boss about her bringing company along on her kitchen raid.

"I'm not laughing at all." At least not outwardly. Inside she was like a kid on an amusement park Tilt-a-Whirl. "I'm giddy because I can't wait to dig into the chipotle tomato cheese spread I heard Chef made up today. He always keeps snacks around for us late-nighters."

In the smaller of the kitchen's three refrigerators, she found the cheese spread and a bottle of wine; the latter she handed to Caleb. After grabbing two saucers, she pointed him to the rack of wineglasses and a bag of seasoned bagel crisps. Then she led him toward the corner of the kitchen where a folding table with four matching chairs was tucked away in a small alcove for the inn's staff to use.

She sat facing the kitchen, which was probably a mistake since it left him to sit facing her and the wall, and left her to deal with his scrutiny. It wouldn't have been awkward had he not just fingered her to orgasm. But he had, and she could hardly ignore how close they'd come to taking things all the way.

Caleb went back to the utensil cabinet for a corkscrew while Miranda removed the cover from the cheese spread and opened the bag of bagel crisps. By the time he had the wine opened and poured, she had used one of the sturdiest chips to scoop cheese onto their plates.

"Do you do this a lot?" he asked. "Midnight snack in the hotel kitchen?"

"Of course." She laughed, dipped a chip half into her cheese. The light in the alcove wasn't as bright as in the main part of the kitchen, making it hard to read his face. "A perk of the job. And a good one since the town is short on all-night convenience stores."

He watched as she popped the bite of food into her mouth. "That's one of my favorite things about New York. The bodegas. Need a sandwich or a roll of toilet paper or batteries at 4:00 a.m.? It's a one-stop shopping trip."

"Is that where you live? New York?"

He shook his head, reached for his wine. "Not anymore."

She noticed he didn't volunteer where he was from. "Do you miss it?"

"Not much to miss." He held her gaze while he drank, and

returned his glass to the table. "I'm there a lot. And I'm in L.A. a lot."

"Is all that travel for work or pleasure?" she asked, doing her best not to look away. His attention was so focused on her, his expression so intense.

"A little of both. I work in…the arts," he said, and she picked up on his hesitation.

The arts could mean books or movies…or music. He'd said he was here for a wedding, one that would be a big deal. She'd gathered from the staff's whispers while they scurried to do Ravyn's bidding that the singer was home. As far as Miranda knew, Brenna had not been in contact with her mother. But with the congressman here as well…

Could Brenna and Teddy be tying the knot? Could Caleb be here because he knew Brenna as an industry insider, or was a friend? She wanted to press for Corinne's sake, but if Brenna didn't want her mother to know what was happening, well, it wasn't Miranda's business anyway.

In fact, she could be totally off the mark. And she was not going to ask questions that could start hurtful rumors. "An interesting line of work, I'll bet."

"It is. It can be. It can also be a pain in the ass."

Now *that* she could relate to. "Show me a career that doesn't have those moments, and I'll show you someone who's not working very hard."

His eyes flashed with a teasing heat. "I know you work hard. I've seen you."

He'd seen things she didn't want to think about right now. She was trying to get beyond the frustration of their aborted encounter, and she never would if every look he gave her reminded her of what they'd done as well as made her regret what she'd missed.

She needed a drink, and took one. "And you want to know what there is about being Candy Cane that could possibly be a pain in the ass."

He popped a bagel chip into his mouth and nodded.

"The wigs make me sweat."

"So why wear them?"

"Because I don't have long red hair, and red is a theme here, in case that's slipped your notice. And, yes, the wigs are well-made and breathable, but that doesn't help much when I'm onstage. Those lights are brutal."

"Then spend more time offstage with the audience."

Funny man. "You'd like that, wouldn't you?"

"Me and the rest of the men watching you. Some of the women, too."

And again the suggestive innuendo, the heat in his eyes, the want. It was hard to look away. "That's what I'm afraid of. And why I don't mingle more than I do. This is a lovers' resort. I don't want to come between the lovers."

"Why did you mingle tonight?"

She'd been trying to figure that out for herself ever since draping herself across his table. Using a broken chip, she toyed with the cheese on her plate.

Instead of eating it, she told him, "You looked lonely."

He paused with his wineglass halfway to his mouth. "A pity kiss?"

"Not hardly," she said, the gruff accusation causing her chest to tighten. "More like a sense of familiarity. Not to sound totally pathetic, but I know that feeling well."

Without drinking, he returned his glass to the table. "And you thought you'd cheer me up."

"To be honest, you weren't the one I was hoping to cheer. My motives were much more selfish." She felt the heat of a blush on her face and fiddled with her food to try to hide it.

"It was my pleasure."

"No," she said, laughing quietly. "I'm pretty sure it was mine. You were the one left hanging."

"Being left hanging never killed a guy." He gave her a look that left her unable to breathe.

Oh, this was going so many places she wouldn't have expected when singing for him tonight, places she wasn't sure she was ready for. "Not according to the stories I've heard."

"Old wives' tales. Trust me. But just to be on the safe side…" He shifted forward, leaning toward her with an intent that wasn't threatening, but unnerved her because of what she sensed he was going to say. "I'll come prepared to tomorrow night's show."

"Thanks. Now I'll never be able to perform," she said, sighing as she popped the chip and cheese into her mouth. It kept her from having to say anything more, and gave her a chance to catch the breath she still hadn't found.

He didn't press, gave her the time, finally asking, "Were you a performer before coming here?"

Reaching for her drink, she cut her gaze sharply toward him. "Is this the man who works in the arts asking?"

He shook his head. "Just the man who kissed you."

And thank goodness he left his comment at the kiss. "Then, no. Not a performer. Unless you count singing in the shower and the church choir."

"A soloist?"

"From time to time. Always at Christmas."

"Do you do anything special for Christmas here?"

"Besides my regular shows? No. Though I do change up the set. Christmas isn't Christmas without Bing Crosby.

Alan's wife is trying to get me to sing at the high school's holiday dance, but I just can't."

"Why not?" he asked, refilling both of their glasses. "Afraid some of the boys might be lonely?"

"Oh, that is so not funny," she said, though she couldn't stifle a laugh. "But, no. I don't take Candy out of Club Crimson. Except to raid the fridge."

He studied his plate, picked up a bagel crisp. "I would think a local celebrity would be in demand."

"In demand for what?" she asked, curious as to how he saw her alter ego. "Mistletoe doesn't have political fund-raisers or charity events. It's too small a community—one of those places where everybody knows your name. Besides," she went on, "I like my privacy. And Candy's not real. She's a fixture here at the inn just like the huge stone fireplace in the lobby and all the knotty-pine tables."

"I disagree. You're not huge or knotty."

"Very funny," she said, tossing a wedge of bagel at his chest, wondering whether to put an end to their evening, or forget sleep and talk to him until morning. She was exhilarated, exhausted.…

When he lifted the bottle to pour her more wine, she found her hand coming up to cover her glass. And there she had her answer. "It's late. Beyond late. And unfortunately, I'm not a woman of leisure."

"Meaning your real self needs to get home so tomorrow you won't fall asleep during brain surgery, or while coming in for an emergency landing, or plowing the back forty, or whatever it is you do when you're not a redhead."

"And that depends on the day of the week," she replied teasingly, wondering what he'd think if he knew about her pedestrian life as a florist. "But, yes, I need to go. This has been the best evening I've had in ages. Thank you."

He followed suit as she got to her feet. "Will I see you tomorrow?"

"If you're in Club Crimson at showtime you will." *You and your condom*. She closed up the bagel crisps, covered the cheese spread, stacked their plates and reached for the wine. "Take this with you."

"Consolation prize?"

She held on to the bottle. "If you're going to be like that, then I'll take it with me and celebrate."

He tossed back his head and laughed. "You, Candy Cane, or whoever you are, are some piece of work."

Good. She was glad he wasn't taking her for granted. "I wouldn't want you to think you could have me without putting in some effort."

He hooked a possessive arm around her neck. "C'mon, mystery woman. Let me walk you back to your dressing room."

She stopped first at the refrigerator, then at the baker's rack, then at the sink where Earnesto took the plates and glasses before waving her and Caleb on their way.

Wearing her sequined gown, her long wavy wig, a warm pair of sheepskin Uggs on her feet and Caleb's jacket over her shoulders, Miranda walked beside him down the hallway from the kitchen to the club. Neither one of them hurried, neither one of them spoke.

It was as if Caleb didn't want to let go of her any more than she wanted to tell him goodnight. They fitted so well as they walked, fitted, too, as they talked. She was certain it would be no different when they made love.

*When.* She was assuming it would happen, rather than ac-cepting they might have nothing but tonight. Counting on more, looking forward to more wasn't smart. Doing so was tantamount to throwing away the past five years she'd spent making a new life. She couldn't do that to herself. She wouldn't do it for a man about whom she knew nothing.

Then they were at her dressing room, the trip over too soon, the silence lingering as she reached out to punch the code into the keypad lock. Caleb stopped her, covering her hand, turning her and pulling her arms above her head as he backed her into the door.

He spread his legs, captured her hips between them, leaned his lower body into hers and rested there. His eyes were fierce, bright, and she was almost unable to draw a breath for thinking about all the things he might want. She scared herself with all the things she wanted.

He lowered his head to the crook of her neck and kissed her there. She raised her chin to give him full access, her nipples tightening with the thrill of the contact. The scratch of his late-night beard over her skin had her sex clenching as she thought of it scraping her belly, her breasts, the skin of her inner thighs.

His mouth was warm, his tongue warmer still, and wet. His hands around her wrists were tight enough to keep her from moving. His erection bulged between them and pressed against her belly.

She wanted to see him naked, to feel him, touch him with her fingers and her lips. She thought about the weight of his cock, the length, the girth, and squirmed where he'd pinned her to the door.

He chuckled, the sound a low rumbling vibration that tickled in the pit of her stomach. She was frustrated, she was aroused, she wanted him, and wiggled her hips to let him know. He laughed again, continued to kiss, to lick, to nibble.

She couldn't take any more. "This isn't enough."

"It has to be," he murmured against her skin, his whiskers and his teeth both torture and bliss.

There were things they could do, ways they could give each other pleasure that wouldn't require a condom. "We can—"

"No, we can't," he said, bruising her at the base of her neck. "Not tonight."

He was doing this on purpose. Making her miserable. Making her ache. Making her wish she had it in her to be reckless. "This isn't fair."

"Life never is."

She groaned. "Don't you want—"

"I do, but I can wait."

She didn't want to wait. She wanted him, and badly enough that throwing caution to the wind, taking a chance…surely it was worth it. There were other options—

Putting an end to her musings, Caleb stepped back, his touch lingering on a lock of her hair. "Good night…Annie."

She rolled her eyes. "It's not Annie."

"Belle."

"Hardly."

"Daisy," he said, skipping from B to D, since Candy filled the C position.

"Uh-uh," she said, grinning to herself as she turned to open the door.

"Erin."

Shaking her head, she laughed. "Nope."

"Fanny."

"Good night, Caleb." And with one hand on the doorknob, she stood on her tiptoes, kissing him on the cheek before backing into her dressing room and closing the door.

She leaned against it, taking a deep breath and trying to remember the last time she'd had this much fun, realizing it had been so long the memory no longer existed.

It was time to change that, to make some new memories that would hold her long after he was gone. She just had to figure out how to make that happen without giving herself away.

# 6

CALEB TOOK THE bottle of wine Candy had given him in the kitchen back to the nightclub's stage and waited just off the hallway in the wings. Best he could tell, there was no exit from Club Crimson other than this one and the main one into the inn's lobby. He figured whoever Candy Cane was, she'd head back through the kitchen to leave.

From here, he could catch a glimpse of her as she made her escape. He wanted to see what she looked like in her glasses and short brown hair, certain from seeing the hairbrush and contact-lens case in her dressing room that she was making the transition from her stage self to her real self even now.

He wasn't going to stalk her or follow her home—he'd be hard-pressed to do the latter since he was here without wheels. And the former, well, showing up for tomorrow night's show was where he drew the line.

But after the time they'd spent together tonight, he was more curious about her than ever. He wanted to glimpse the woman who had turned him on, the woman he knew he was going to have trouble getting out of his head. This rarely happened. No, it never happened, he mused, lifting the wine bottle and thinking back over his thirty-seven years.

Sure, there'd been women, lovers who'd lasted for months,

one in college he'd stayed with for almost two years. Nix that. One who'd stayed with him for almost two years. He hadn't made the change, she had. She hadn't liked that he'd had a mistress—journalism—that had demanded his time, his energy, his love.

He'd been obsessed with learning the world of news reporting, with researching, finding one lead and following it down a rabbit hole to another, with pushing public and private boundaries, while serving both his audience and the subjects of the pieces he wrote.

Women he'd dated after his college sweetheart dumped him had felt the same way about his split loyalties, so he'd quit dating and settled for one-night stands, the occasional fling, and sex with his own right hand.

Instead of fighting the Mars–Venus wars, he'd poured his emotions into his work. No need putting himself through the wringer when it was obvious he was worthless at balancing the things he loved.

Caleb was just about to fall into a pit of self-pity when he heard Candy open her door. Leaving the wine bottle on the floor against the wall, he edged as far as he dared toward the steps that descended from the wings into the hallway.

The light in front of her dressing room wasn't the greatest, but it would've been bright enough for him to see her by— if she hadn't already pulled the hood of her parka over her head and been looking straight down, her face completely obscured.

Carrying a small red gym bag and wearing her padded boots, what looked like insulated sweatpants and the coat, she checked that the door had locked behind her, then headed toward the kitchen as Caleb had hoped.

He'd pulled off his boots while waiting, knowing they'd

make too much noise should he have to follow to get the look he wanted. He set off now to do just that, keeping his distance while keeping her in sight.

The kitchen was empty and dark save for one light left on at each end. He breathed in dish soap and floor cleaner and the lingering odors of fresh fruit and garlic, hanging back as she hugged the perimeter of the room.

On the other side, she hit a button that opened a secured door. She walked through, and Caleb rushed forward, his socks sliding on the floor as he caught the handle before it latched. He waited several seconds, finally slipping into what turned out to be a large storage room where a big red exit sign glowed on the far wall.

This room was colder, filled with shelves of boxed supplies, freezers, laundry carts and crates of booze. The way out—to which Candy was headed—looked as if it led to a delivery bay where trucks could pull in at the rear of the inn to unload, and Caleb assumed the staff parking lot was adjacent. He could hardly follow her all the way outside, but he saw a window in the heavy steel door he could look through.

He ducked behind the closest shelving unit and listened to the pad of her footsteps echo in the cavernous space. Since she'd kept his jacket, leaving him in his shirt sleeves, he rubbed his hands up and down his arms for warmth while waiting for her to reach her destination.

Once she'd slammed her hand against the red button that released the exit's lock, Caleb took off after her. By the time he got to the door, it had closed, and the room was again secure. He eased up to the window and peered through.

Snow swirled lightly in the parking lot. He could see her form as she hurried toward her car, and he watched her fumble to get her key in the lock, then fumble again to get the driver's-side door open.

After starting the engine, she let it warm, turning on her headlights and sitting there for several minutes. Caleb imagined her cupping her hands together, blowing into them, her breath frosting the air.

Just thinking about it made him cold. Standing on the concrete floor in his socks didn't help. He tugged on his boots then looked out in time to see her drive away, the older import jerking as she shifted the gears, exhaust belching out in wispy clouds.

Shivering, he continued to stand there until she disappeared into the night, then stuffed his hands in his jeans pockets, hunched his shoulders and hurried back to the other side of the room.

He returned to the door that led into the kitchen—and that's when he saw the keypad on the wall beside it. He tried the handle, got nothing. He looked for a phone, found one that rang directly to security.

It was either call for help and look like a fool, spend the next few hours in here until the kitchen staff arrived for the morning shift, or leave the same way Candy whoever-she-was had done and traipse in his street clothes—no jacket, no hat, no gloves—around to the front of the inn.

None of the options thrilled him, but the third would get him back to his room a whole lot faster. He glanced in the laundry carts and lucked out, finding a blanket wadded up in the bottom of one.

Wrapping it around his shoulders like a super-reporter's cape, he damned himself for being so nosy, and headed out into the frigid winter night for a much deserved—and self-inflicted—comeuppance.

IT WAS NEARLY 3:00 a.m. when Miranda climbed into bed. She couldn't remember the last time she'd been so exhausted. The shows she did four nights a week tired her already. Adding to the mix the extra hours spent tonight with Caleb, her sexual release and her mad dash to escape, well, she barely had the strength to set her alarm.

She had no idea why Caleb had waited for her, or why he'd followed her, especially when it was obvious that he had no intention of catching her. That left her wondering, as she drifted between wakefulness and sleep, if he'd discovered what he'd been after. Wondering, too, with no small amount of amusement, if he'd found a way out of the warehouse. Or if he was still huddled up somewhere in the room.

She was so glad she'd considered the possibility of his being there—whether to give persuading her to come up to his room one more shot, or to convince her that it would be worth her while to take him home—and had pulled up her parka's hood before stepping out into the hallway.

She would've preferred that he respect her privacy and her wish to remain incognito, but she understood his testosterone-driven need to be in control. That didn't mean she was going to let him find her out, or to score more points in this game than he had with his promise to come prepared to tomorrow night's show.

How in the world she was going to get through her performance… She shivered, pulled her comforter to her chin and settled back on her bed's mountain of pillows, refusing to borrow trouble and think about that now.

She borrowed trouble of a different kind instead. Last-minute thoughts of how much differently the night would've played out had one of them had a condom meant her dreams were filled with graphically detailed images—his body, her body, fingers and tongues, and, oh, how he kissed.

She woke late and not the least bit rested, her body way oversensitive as she showered and dressed. Breakfast was a cup of coffee in a travel mug and a toasted English muffin that, by the time her car had warmed up enough to make it to the shop, was as cold as the blackberry jelly topping it.

The snow flurries that had swirled around her during last night's drive home were gone this morning. The sun was shining brightly, reflecting off the blanket of white and forcing her to reach for the sunglasses clipped to her visor.

The town's one plow had been out early, and the trip from her bungalow to the store was uneventful—a good thing since she was having trouble letting go of last night and focusing on the roads. Running a half hour late didn't help.

The part of her brain not thinking about Caleb was thinking about the work she had ahead. A fairly large order had come in last week, well, large by Under the Mistletoe standards. And now that she thought about it…

The flowers had to be for the same wedding Caleb was here for. There were two standing floral arrangements, one for either side of the altar in the chapel at the inn, a bridal bouquet and one for the single attendant, as well as an exquisite corsage for the mother of the bride, and boutonnieres for the groom and best man.

The name on the order was neither Eagleton nor Black, nor was it Sparks, but if Brenna and the congressman were here to get married, that would make perfect sense. They'd be keeping their plans as hush-hush as possible, using assistants to run errands and see to the details of the event.

And though most brides were very hands-on when it came to the decorations for the ceremony, Miranda understood Brenna keeping Corinne in the loop by having her mother help with the flowers—even if Corinne didn't know that's what she was doing.

Brenna had made it more than clear that she wanted to reconcile, sending birthday and Christmas gifts—which Corinne gave away—trying to reimburse the money she'd taken—money Corinne, as generous as she was, couldn't see beyond her pride to keep—calling and leaving messages Corinne never returned.

It came as no surprise that Corinne was already at Under the Mistletoe when Miranda sneaked in the back door at ten-thirty. The older woman looked up from where she was trimming stems and arranging red roses in a delivery box with silver and gold ribbons. "Late night?"

Her employee's simple question cleared Miranda's mind of everything but her time with Caleb, and she couldn't help blurting it out. "I met a man."

"Oh, really?" Like Miranda, Corinne was divorced and held out little hope that as long as she lived in Mistletoe, her marital status would change. "Long-term potential or short-term fling?"

"Definitely fling-worthy," Miranda admitted. "But since he's just visiting, I'd have to say—"

"A fling is all it will be," Corinne finished for her.

And such was Miranda's lot in life. She sighed, tucked her purse away in her locker and pulled on the red and green apron she wore to protect her clothes.

"If I were a less practical woman, I'd say the Fates were playing an unnecessarily cruel joke. I mean, I hardly need to be reminded that I'm living in a town that caters to lovers, and have little chance of having one of my own. Or having one for longer than a fling anyway."

She stopped as the truth consumed her. "Not that I've even had one of those since I've been here—"

"But one can always hope," Corinne said as she assembled the top of the flower box and fitted it over the bottom, tucking the order ticket between the two parts. "Did he say how long he'll be in town? Or what he's doing here? I need to know how many mornings I'm going to have to take up your slack."

"Ha." Miranda stuck out her tongue in response to her friend's teasing. "He didn't say how long, no, and I won't be late again. As for what he's doing here—" All her speculation about Brenna returned, but since she had no proof, or any business gossiping about the girl to her mother…

"Well?" Corinne prompted, her brown eyes curious, the blond highlights in her shoulder-length hair making her look younger than her fifty-three years.

Miranda forged ahead, sharing none of her thoughts so as not to influence any conclusions Corinne might draw. "He said he's here for a wedding."

"The same wedding we're doing the flowers for?"

"I have a feeling it could be. He did say the ceremony was private, but it would be a pretty big deal once word of the nuptials got out."

Color rising on her cheeks, Corinne shoved the box of roses at Miranda, averting her gaze as she moved from the worktable to her order book, set next to the phone. "Then I'd better get busy, hadn't I? Wouldn't want our flowers to reflect poorly on any big deal."

Miranda looked down at the box she held. She had no way of knowing what Corinne was thinking, but judging by the other woman's reaction, it was quite likely word had reached her that Brenna was staying at the inn.

Miranda set the box on the table, and pulled open a drawer beneath the work surface where spools of ribbon hung on built-in dowels. "I'm hardly worried about your work reflecting poorly on anything or anyone, but if you'd rather I tackle the wedding, you can work on Mayor Flynn's dinner party."

Corinne didn't respond. She stood and watched Miranda measure a length of Christmas plaid ribbon to tie around the box. "Marvetta Chance told me yesterday that Barry picked up Teddy Eagleton at the airport."

"Hmm."

"I asked Patrice when she dropped off Zoe after choir practice last night if it was true that Brenna was in town."

"What did she say?" Miranda asked, expecting Alan's wife to be more circumspect than the inn's shuttle driver.

"Nothing, but then we both know that Patrice treats the comings and goings at the inn the way a priest treats his confessional."

Miranda didn't want to butt in on Corinne's personal life, but the two of them had been friends long enough that she felt she owed it to the other woman to say her piece. "It's not any of my business, but isn't it possible that if Brenna is marrying Teddy, she's having the wedding here because she wants you to come?"

"More like she wants to rub my nose in it. 'Look, Ma! I can take money from you and take Teddy from his wife and there's nothing you can do to stop me.'" Shaking her head, Corinne moved closer to hold the ribbon in place while Miranda fashioned the bow. "I just pray to God her sister doesn't find out that she's here."

At that point, Miranda figured it was best to move on. "When's the last time Zoe saw her?"

Corinne gave a careless shrug. "Brenna picked her up after school on her birthday last year. She took her to Denver for the weekend. Spoiled her rotten." Corinne grabbed the box of flowers and headed from the back room to the front of the shop, tossing over her shoulder, "But trust me—if I have my way? She'll never see Brenna again."

Frowning, Miranda followed. "You can't mean that."

"I can. I do. Zoe has her whole life ahead of her. She doesn't need to get involved in her sister's, or end up being dragged through the mud Brenna seems to enjoy wallowing in."

The gossips had had a Britney-esque field day with Ravyn Black's comings and goings. Having suffered similarly, Miranda believed Brenna might truly be in need of her mother's understanding.

But with Corinne still nursing the old hurt, it was hard to imagine anything but a miracle bringing the two Sparks women together.

# 7

STILL TIRED, still cold and still hungry, Caleb followed the hostess to the quiet table he'd requested against the back wall of One in Vermillion. The pub was the more casual of the inn's two restaurants, the other being Will Ruby Mine.

This whole red thing was still getting on his nerves, but today his pique had less to do with the resort thematically exploiting the concept of love and romance, and more to do with a woman who was hiding behind red costumes and red hair.

He had a feeling Candy whoever-she-was had known exactly what she was doing when she'd led him into the storage room and left him locked in there. And he'd deserved it. He should've left well enough alone. Any other man would've done so, would've respected her privacy and waited for her to reveal herself in good time.

Caleb wasn't any other man. He was a journalist. Curiosity was in his blood. And he didn't have good time. He was due, in fact, to leave immediately following the Saturday-evening wedding. Or, he had been until, on his way to meet Ravyn, he'd stopped by the front desk to extend his stay.

Not an easy feat to accomplish with the inn booked solid so near the holidays, but possession being nine-tenths of the law and money being no object, he'd managed to hang on to his room through the weekend, though only by the skin of his teeth.

Come Monday morning, it was either hit the road for the airport and his rescheduled flight, or head down the mountain, find less colorful lodging, and rent a car to get him back and forth, since he doubted Candy whoever-she-was would be inviting him to her place for home cooking anytime soon.

Home cooking he could do without. Hell, if it came right down to it, he'd even survive not taking her to bed. He wasn't looking forward to things going that way, but, as he'd told her, no man ever died from being hung out to dry when the sex thing didn't work out with a woman.

It was leaving here without knowing who she was that was giving him the true hard time. And not because of thinking he knew her. He wanted to know the woman who had kissed a stranger in a nightclub as if that moment meant more than the rest of her show.

The kiss, the intimacy, the near miss in her dressing room. He still couldn't believe she had given herself to him so freely. He wanted to chalk it up to being an extension of the whole lovers'-resort thing, but Candy whoever-she-was had seemed knocked for a loop of her own.

He couldn't leave here without discovering more about her—which presented a real problem. He no longer trusted himself to keep private what was told to him in confidence, to separate the personal of Caleb from the business of Max. And with his believing that Candy had secrets…

"Mr. McGregor?"

He looked up, expecting his server with his coffee, frowning that it hadn't arrived. Instead he saw a young woman, a kid really, dressed like so many others in low-rise jeans, brightly colored insulated boots, her hair caught back in a bandana, not a hint of makeup on her face.

"Yes?"

"I'm Brenna Sparks. We have an appointment."

"We do?" He wasn't firing on all cylinders, but he knew he should be able to place the name.

She rolled her eyes, then stared, waiting, as if his study of her would bring recognition. When it didn't, she tossed back her head, reached for the neckline of the top she wore layered over several others and ripped it with the loud banshee wail made famous online in bootlegged Evermore concert videos.

Okay, not a kid. Not a typical congressman's wife either. Brenna Sparks was Ravyn Black. Hard to believe this woman who looked about twelve years old was to Congressman Teddy Eagleton what Marilyn Monroe had been to JFK. Was more, actually, since they were about to become one.

"Sorry," he said, getting to his feet, and gesturing toward the chair opposite his, glancing at the other patrons, who were obviously not banshee fans. "Please, sit. I'm still trying to wake up."

She gave him a look that was decidedly maternal and not kidlike at all. "It's almost noon."

He shrugged, amused to have a rock star criticize his sleeping habits. "One of those nights. What can I say?"

She plopped into the chair, reached for his water glass, and downed half of it before looking up. "You can say I'm not making a big mistake by telling my story to a half-wit."

He caught sight of the server approaching and signaled for another coffee before taking his seat. "You're not, and I'm not. I was just lost in thought, trying to find a solution to the problem that kept me up so late."

The server returned then, setting cups and saucers and a pitcher of cream on the table, handing them both menus and explaining the specials of the day while Brenna studied the appetizer section.

Listening with only half an ear, Caleb reached inside the jacket he wore, finding his digital recorder in that pocket, his pen and notebook in the one at his hip.

"I'll let you look over your menus, and be back in a few for your orders," said the young man in black pants with a white shirt and red tie.

He had just turned to go when Brenna stopped him. "Would you go ahead and bring an order of crab cakes?" She looked at Caleb, who shook his head. "That's all for now."

"I'll get that turned right in."

Caleb waited until they were alone, then asked, "Do you mind if I record our conversation? I take notes, but a recorder makes for better accuracy."

She reached for the device, activated the record function and brought the microphone to her mouth. "And we know reporters are always accurate."

He didn't want to have that argument now. "You've given him the exclusive and Max takes that seriously. He doesn't want any mistakes. Having your voice on a digital file detailing your relationship with the congressman is about as accurate as it gets."

"Whatever." She handed back the recorder with a shrug. "Let's just get this done. I've got a facial and a massage at three."

Caleb took the device and left it running, studying his companion while she spent longer than he would've expected focused on the menu. The server returned then with Brenna's crab cakes and took her order for a large baked potato with the works. Caleb didn't care what he ate, so he ordered the same.

She insisted Caleb share the appetizer. He did, and once he'd bit in, was glad. "This is what I love about being on assignment."

"Having crab cakes for lunch?"

"Breakfast, lunch, dinner or midnight snack."

"I'm assuming you travel with a gastroenterologist?"

"Just a pharmacy's worth of meds."

She snorted, forked up another bite of her food, and they chatted about nothing for several minutes. Brenna finally asked, "So where do you want to start? What do you want to know? How Teddy and I met, or wedding details, or juicy news on the next album?"

He wanted it all, but waited while the server delivered the football-size potatoes with pools of melted butter, sour cream, cheese, chives and bacon. His stomach rumbled. "I saw the congressman in the lobby yesterday."

Her look said he could do better than that. "It's a wedding. I'm the bride. He's the groom."

"Is he still not crazy about a media witness to your vows?" Caleb asked, dredging a bite of potato through the reservoir of melted butter.

She sipped at the soda she'd called back the server to get her. "Not crazy about the media being Max Savage, no. But he agrees it's better to do it this way than to have helicopters hovering over a beach in Maui, or to have dozens of half-assed contradictory reports springing up and causing him unnecessary grief. Not that it won't happen anyway—"

"But at least there will be digital proof if you need it."

"Exactly."

"I'm sure he gets as much of that in his position as you do in the band."

Placing her fork on the edge of her plate, she sat back and rolled her head on her shoulders as if gathering her thoughts, sorting through, shaking off those she didn't want to share. When she faced him again, he saw confusion more than confidence, and that intrigued him as much as her confession.

"We love what we do," she said. "The band and I. We're devoted to what we do. We believe in the messages of our songs. It's a heart-and-soul thing for us."

She looked down at her plate, a little girl with hurt feelings. "But that's not what gets written about in reviews. That's never the focus of articles about the music. Sound bites are always played back in a negative context. And, yes, I know that's what I signed on for when I chose this life."

She might have expected some of what was written about Evermore, but he doubted she or the band members had anticipated the vitriolic charges that their lyrics encouraged drug use, casual sex, teen rebellion and even suicide pacts. Nothing new in the world of rock 'n' roll, but amplified because of their explosive Internet presence.

As Max Savage, Caleb had written about all of these things. He'd also quoted disillusioned fans who said Ravyn's affair with the charismatic conservative congressman was akin to selling out. That it proved she didn't stand by her message of being true to oneself at all.

"You know the public thinks the only reason you're with Teddy is to legitimize your act. Make it acceptable to the mainstream. How can parents complain about their children listening to Evermore if Congressman Eagleton, their contemporary, puts his stamp of approval on the band?"

"That's such bullshit," Brenna said, shaking her head. "Teddy's generation grew up with Def Leppard and Poison as their music idols. My generation grew up with Marilyn Manson and Nine Inch Nails. They turned out fine, we turned out fine. Today's kids, my sister's age group, they'll turn out fine, too. It's not about the music. It's about knowing yourself, who you are, what you want."

He couldn't believe she was that naive, or even worse, that

he was feeling a twinge of something uncomfortable over his part in the grief she'd suffered from the reports in the press.

He shook it off, asking, "And you think kids in your sister's age group know those things? Who they are? What they want? That they're not influenced by Evermore singing about putting an end to the pain?"

Having picked up her fork earlier, Brenna now tossed it to the table and plopped back in her chair. "I love how those lyrics are the ones everyone pulls out of context without paying any attention to what comes before or what follows."

"More negative sound bites?"

"What do you think?" she asked, holding up one hand to keep him from answering.

Caleb watched as she closed her eyes, squirmed in her chair until she was comfortable, then reached for the torn edges of her top. She held tightly to the fabric, her knuckles nearly white, her chest rising and falling.

And then she sang, pouring her emotions into the lyrics she'd written, telling her audience that life was hard and lonely, that escape was just moments away. That an end to the pain could be had by reaching out, and that if one did, the loneliness would all go away.

She fell silent then, took a deep shuddering breath and then opened her eyes. They were red, her lower lids brimming with tears, the emotional resonance of the words she'd poured out unmistakable, undeniable—to her, and to the crowd who got to their feet and applauded.

Caleb couldn't help but be moved.

Looking down at her plate, Brenna reached for her fork again and whispered, "I sing about reaching out. How can anyone say those lyrics are destructive?"

He had no answer. But as the noise in the pub died down,

he realized that what he'd said earlier about the parents of her fans had hit a deep nerve. And with Brenna mentioning her younger sister…

"Did you and Teddy get together because you thought a relationship with the congressman would persuade your mother to accept what you're doing with your life?"

"If my mother and I were estranged because of my music, taking Teddy home for Christmas dinner might have softened her up, but since my music isn't the problem between us, I'd have to say no."

Interesting. "What is the problem between you?"

Bristling, Brenna cut him off. "If you want this interview to continue, don't ask me about that again."

So there *was* more to that story. He'd come back to it later. For now… "Then let's talk about your groom. The first time you met. The heat you've both taken over the months. The impact that has had on your relationship. The impact your relationship has had on the band."

They spent the next two hours talking about the things the public was going to be glued to their televisions to find out. A lot of what Brenna told him, Caleb already knew to be fact. Other things he'd suspected, but had not been able to verify.

But there was even more that surprised him. Her vulnerability, for one thing. He didn't know why. He did know it shouldn't. The impenetrable, unflappable persona of Evermore's lead singer was an act the same way Max Savage was an act. The same way Candy Cane was an act.

Why he expected the woman who wore Ravyn's hard shell to be anything but who she was, singing her heart out in the middle of the pub, digging into her baked potato and crab cakes and then ordering key lime pie for dessert, made no sense.

He knew there was very little of importance in what he

wrote about for his column. Or in what the paparazzi captured and then a voice-over artist narrated for the nightly Max Savage segment of televised entertainment news. All of that was surface. The truth was found in the layers beneath, the layers she was exposing and trusting him not to exploit.

As Brenna talked and he listened, picking up on the nuances in her voice and questioning her in depth during those moments when her guard was down, he found his mind drifting to the layers of Candy Cane and what *she* might be hiding.

Why did she perform in costume and use an alter ego? Was it all about the act and the theme of the inn? Or was it about protecting her true identity? He knew why he didn't reveal himself, but Candy whoever-she-was didn't have the same limelight to avoid.

Her stage was small, her audience limited to lovers who gave her but a fraction of their attention. It wasn't as though her risk of exposure held a candle to his...unless she was hiding more than the woman who lived in Mistletoe. Unless, like Brenna, she had something painful in her past that she didn't want discovered.

"Is that all?"

"One more thing," Caleb said, forcing his mind from Candy and her many personas and back to the woman with multiple personalities who was at hand. He probed where he knew he shouldn't, but where as a journalist he had to. He wanted to tell all of her story and he wanted to tell it right.

"What happened between you and your mother?"

Brenna's expression froze, her body stiffened. "I told you not to go there."

"I know," he said. "But it's what I do."

She got to her feet, retrieved her napkin from the floor and tossed it onto the table. "Then you need to learn to stop."

He'd be stopping soon enough. But he had this one last story to tell, this one last chance to do penance. "Will your family be at the wedding?"

Her only answer was the finger she gave him before walking away.

# 8

"WHO IS IT?" Miranda called in response to the knock on her dressing-room door. She was still wearing her sweats and her glasses, not to mention her own head of hair. After her successful escape from Caleb last night, there was no way she was opening the door to him now and undoing that victory.

"It's Patrice."

Thank goodness. "Hey, sweetie. C'mon in."

Alan's wife pushed open the door, came inside and leaned back, making sure with a quick test of the knob that it locked behind her. Miranda noticed, but didn't comment. Patrice obviously wanted privacy.

The other woman's nearly black hair hung in a long braid over one shoulder. She wore leather work boots, faded jeans and a cable-knit sweater in a herringbone pattern of black and green. The look was as much a uniform as the one she wore on the slopes as a member of the ski patrol team.

"What're you doing here so late in the day?" Miranda asked, getting a closer look at the flush on her friend's usually creamy complexion as she sat on the bench beside her.

Patrice's eyes went wide. "Tell me about your new man. I want to hear everything. I am starved for gossip. There has been nothing going on at work. No avalanches. No crashes. No one to rescue. No lost hikers to find."

Gossip. On one hand, the bane of Miranda's existence, on the other, a source of fun between girlfriends that she glee-fully—if hypocritically—participated in. "Who have you been getting your info from? Alan or Corinne?"

"Both, actually, though Corinne didn't know enough to juice things up, and Alan's a man and thinks juice comes in a jar." Patrice nudged her shoulder against Miranda's when she laughed. "So? Is he juicy?"

Miranda met the other woman's reflection in the mirror. "Juicy enough, but there's not a lot to tell. I kissed him during my set—"

Patrice gasped. "You what?"

"Tell me about it." Miranda gave a moan and a nod. "It was so strange. It was the end of the night, I was in the crowd for the last song and there he was. Alone. The only person in the club alone. One of the only people I've ever seen in there alone."

"So you kissed him? Because he was alone?"

And how stupid did it sound to hear it said? "Trust me. I've tried to find an answer that makes more sense."

"No luck, I guess?" Patrice leaned forward and grabbed one of Miranda's lipsticks, twisting it open and frowning at the shade. "What do you think?"

"I think it would look great. And, no. No luck." She watched her friend lean closer to the mirror and carefully apply the dark coral. "A man alone is no reason for me to risk ruining the life I've built here."

"Who says? A man alone is probably the perfect reason to risk it. I mean, it's a fling. It's not like he'll be here long enough to ruin anything." Patrice pursed her lips, smiled, pressed them together and made a loud pop. "I wonder if Alan will like this."

Knowing the other woman rarely wore makeup at all,

Miranda considered her visitor's complexion. "You could add some color to your eyes for balance."

"Are you calling me unbalanced?" Patrice asked with a frown.

Miranda grinned. "Just your face."

"Gee, thanks." Patrice found one of Miranda's headbands and pulled her long wispy bangs away from her eyes. "But I'm serious, you know."

"About the risk?"

"Sure. You've been here five years. You haven't dated. The East Coast divorce gossip has surely died down by now. What's the harm in having anyone you once knew find out that you're living here? If anything's ruining your life, it's you being so careful." Patrice cut her gaze to Miranda's reflected one. "I mean, five years without getting laid? How can you stand it?"

She'd stood it because there hadn't been men here to date, and because she stayed too busy to leave and find one. True, she had probably taken being cautious way too far. At the beginning it had been a necessity. Then it had become habit. Now it was a rut she didn't see a way out of—especially with this new looming threat of the retrial.

Looking back with twenty-twenty hindsight, it was easy to see that she could've handled things with less emotion and more logic. But here she was. And things really hadn't been *that* bad. Or if they had been, she'd done a good job of lying to herself. She turned back to Patrice.

"Now that Marshall's in the news again? If it were made known that the ex-Mrs. Gordon was living in a lovers' resort in the Rocky Mountains, reporters would fall all over themselves booking flights and rooms."

"But I still don't get what that has to do with you having a fling here in Mistletoe."

"I don't want the man I have a fling with to leave here, see coverage of Marshall's trial, and when the mystery of the ex-wife who's dropped out of sight comes up, to then call the press and say, 'Hey, I know where she is. I just boinked her silly.'"

Patrice stopped short of rolling her eyes. "Do you think that's what will happen?"

"Am I borrowing trouble, you mean?" Miranda shrugged. "Probably, but I've been doing the better-safe-than-sorry thing for so long, it's instinct. And knock on wood, it's worked."

"Worked to keep you from getting laid, anyway." Patrice picked up an eyeshadow quad, then discarded the selection of blues for one with greens. "Doesn't it get to you?"

"It does. At times." Too many to name. "Like when watching Bridget Jones kiss Mark Darcy."

Patrice, a hater of anything labeled romantic or comedy, groaned. "Back to your better-safe-than-sorry lifestyle. *My* instincts are telling me that you need to ditch it and have an affair with the juicy one while he's here."

*Juicy.* The thought had everything in Miranda tingling. "Since it was only the lack of a condom that kept us from doing it last night, I'd say there's a good possibility."

"You!" Patrice pointed at Miranda's reflection with the eyeshadow brush she held. "What have I told you about buying condoms when you buy tampons?"

Ridiculously, Miranda's face heated. "If I bought condoms every time I bought tampons, I'd have enough to keep me through menopause."

"And if you'd bought them at least once, you'd be all kinds of sore and hobbling around today." Patrice finished dusting on a glittery sea-green shadow before adding a darker pine color in the creases of her lids. "I'm hoping Alan will start tearing off my clothes once he sees the new me and then I'll be all kinds of sore and hobbling. He does know the code to your door lock, right?"

"Uh-uh. No way. If you're planning on getting naked in my dressing room while I'm singing, stop. Having Caleb in the audience will be enough of a distraction. Thinking about you in here with Alan would put me over the edge."

"Caleb," Patrice said, as if weighing the name on her tongue. "I like it. What's he like? Where's he from? What does he do? Why's he here all alone?"

"I don't know where he's from. He never said, though I'm thinking the East Coast. As far as what he's like, well, he's attentive and sexy and very nice. Not pushy. A great kisser. A great flirt. And, I hope, a good sport."

"Why's that?"

"When I left last night, he followed me."

"All the way home?"

Miranda shook her head. "Just down the hall, through the kitchen and warehouse to the parking lot."

"To your car?"

"Not quite that far," Miranda said, remembering the blur of Caleb's face as he'd watched her drive away. "The last time I saw him, he was looking out the window of the exit door. I left him there."

"You left him in the warehouse?" Patrice asked, and when Miranda grinned, nearly screeched. "Oh my God! Do you think he stayed in there all night?"

"I'm going to guess that when he realized he couldn't get back in the way he'd come out without calling security, he walked around to the front of the inn."

"And froze his ass off." Laughing, Patrice closed up the eyeshadow and found a new mascara in the vanity's top drawer. She pumped the wand in and out of the tube then swept the brush over her lashes. "You know, when you sleep with him—"

"You mean *if*."

"*When* you sleep with him, you're going to have to consider more than having enough condoms. Do you wear your contacts?" One stroke of mascara. "Do you wear your glasses?" Another stroke. "Do you wear a wig?" A third stroke. "Do you wear your real hair?" A fourth.

"Yeah. I've gone over all of those a thousand times."

"And?"

"Do I want a one- or two-night stand?" Miranda opened one palm for one option, opened the other for a second. "Or do I want more? I mean, if sex is the goal, why get out of any more than my underwear?"

"Because nothing beats full-body contact?"

"Okay, so I get out of everything but my hair." She flipped the ends of the wig she would be wearing tonight; it sat on the vanity, still fitted to its foam head form. "We can have sex in here up against the wall or on the floor or on the vanity bench."

"True."

"But if we have dinner or drinks and get to know each other, and things look promising, do I sleep with him as Candy? Or as the real me? And how much of the real me do I really want him to know?" Miranda felt her voice and her blood pressure both rising. "Miranda Kelly who owns Under the Mistletoe? Or the ex-Miranda Gordon who lived in Baltimore and was married to Marshall, the crook?"

Patrice wrapped an arm around Miranda's shoulder and hugged her close. "Why don't you play it by ear, sweetie? Take it a day at a time."

"That's all well and good, except I can't think he's going to be here for very many," Miranda said, deflating.

"You never told me *why* he's here," Patrice said, getting back to her makeup.

"He's here for a wedding."

"Do we know whose?"

"No." Miranda paused, waited until she had her friend's attention, and added, "But Teddy and Brenna are both here."

Patrice's eyes widened. "Are you kidding?"

"Corinne knew. I thought you probably did, too."

"Nope. I've been wrapped up with the Christmas dance plans. And trying to get someone to sing. Someone besides Zoe," she added before Miranda could make the suggestion. "She's already on the program. I wanted someone with a little more...cachet."

Which Patrice thought Miranda had. "So ask Brenna."

"Are you kidding? Corinne would defriend me forever. God, I can't imagine what she must be going through. This whole congressman–rock-star thing has been a nightmare since the beginning. I can't believe they might be getting married."

Miranda reached for her sponge and foundation to get started on her face. "Actually, having both of her daughters onstage at the dance might be the very thing to bring about a reconciliation. Unless there is a wedding and it magically happens there."

"If only life was that easy."

"Worth giving it a shot?"

Patrice got to her feet, and with Miranda's nod of permission, pocketed both the eyeshadow quad and the mascara. "Let me run it by Alan. And thanks for the makeover."

"If there's anything else you want, run it by him while you look like a runway model."

"More like a sportsman's catalog model. But then Alan

does like a woman with a bulls-eye for his arrow to hit," Patrice said, laughing as she opened the door.

"Just keep all that shooting out of my dressing room," Miranda called after her friend who yelled back, "Break a leg, and then you won't have to worry about it!"

# 9

AN HOUR BEFORE THE SHOW, Caleb was at the bar in Club Crimson nursing a glass of sparkling water with lime. No more booze for him until he had a better handle on Candy. He was going to be one-hundred-percent sober for tonight's show.

And as far as how things would go down after the show? For that, he'd come prepared—and then some. They could make love until his plane took off on Monday without having to worry about being protected.

Strangely, he hadn't thought a lot about Candy this afternoon. He'd been focused on writing the copy for the wedding story, and on Brenna Sparks and her estrangement from her mother. He'd wondered what that might have to do with her choice of Mistletoe for the event. He couldn't see any other reason for the venue.

For a ceremony so small, she and Teddy could have found the same privacy in any judge's chambers, and then dealt with the media aftermath similarly to how they'd be dealing with it now. But as curious as he was, he let it go. Brenna had told him to drop it, and he had a newfound respect for boundaries.

Only when his stomach had reminded him that his brain needed more fuel than a crab cake and stuffed baked potato had he pushed away from his laptop and ordered room service. After eating and noticing the time, he'd showered away the exhaustion of his work, dressed and headed down to Club Crimson.

He was too early for Candy's show, but that was fine. It allowed him time to really see where she worked. He'd been too tired from traveling and too toasted from drinking to notice much of anything last night.

Er, anything except the overwhelming and sappy color scheme which hadn't improved with either time or sobriety. When he arrived, the club was already half-full, the patrons lulled by piped-in mood music—instrumental pieces, classic crooners, even sexy R & B tunes and pop ballads. Servers worked the room, their trays laden with cocktails, bubbly champagne, even mugs of beer.

Partners in hushed conversations cuddled closer on love seats and sofas. A group of three couples had pulled club chairs into a circle, and were sharing several bottles of wine while boisterously discussing a recent bestseller, politics, the chances of the teams headed for the Superbowl.

Other couples sat in the more privately situated booths— the last in the row the one where Caleb had sat last night— and if they were talking at all, no one could hear. Neither did anyone pay them attention unless they signaled for service.

Tonight, Caleb sat at the far end of the bar, choosing a stool on the short side of the L and putting his back to the wall. From here, he could see the stage and all of the room, save for the few tables behind him.

But the best part was that unlike the back corner booth, the bar was too tall for Candy to drape herself over should she want to slide into his lap and kiss him. Yeah, he wanted her to kiss him, but he didn't want her to start something here in public that they'd have to put on hold.

When she kissed him, when he kissed her, he wanted privacy, no audience, no reason to stop or pull back because the time and place were wrong. Her dressing room was fine. His room upstairs was fine. If she wanted to take him home with her, that, too, was fine. Club Crimson, the lovers' lounge in the lovers' resort in the lovers' town of Mistletoe was not in the least bit fine.

"Can I get you a refill on that? Something stronger, maybe?"

He looked up at the bartender who seemed to be considering him too closely. "The water's fine, but a refill would be good, thanks."

The other man, probably close to Caleb's age with a skier's ruddy tan, returned with the drink himself rather than sending it with one of the servers in their short flirty red skirts. "Here ya go."

"Appreciate it," Caleb said, then waited for the man to walk away. He didn't, and it wasn't hard to know what was coming. The bartender had been hovering last night even before Candy had invited Caleb back to her dressing room. Might as well set his mind at ease. "I left her as safe and sound as I found her. No need to worry, okay?"

The bartender laughed, held out his hand. "Alan Price."

"Caleb McGregor. I'm going to guess that you and Candy whoever-she-is go way back, and you enjoy playing big brother."

"We grew up here, next door to each other. But as far as playing big brother, I'm a friend. That's all."

Hmm. Then this was her home. "A friend who wants to make sure she doesn't invite the wrong creep to her dressing room."

"Last I looked, that's what friends were for."

Nodding, Caleb reached for his water. "She's…not what I expected."

Alan arched a brow, and slid a new napkin beneath Caleb's drink. "What did you expect?"

Caleb shrugged. "A lot of performers continue their act offstage. I didn't find that to be the case with her at all. She was very down-to-earth. Very real. Very nice." And very, very sexy.

"She is. All of that."

"And you want to make sure I don't hurt her. That all my intentions are good."

Alan leaned a hand on the bar and looked down as if fighting a smile. "I doubt, in Candy's case, you and I would agree on what makes a good intention."

Caleb was pretty sure the other man had that right. He was pretty sure, too, that his intentions were his own business. "Do you call her Candy in private?"

Alan laughed. "If you think I'm going to tell you her name, think again."

"I don't think that at all," Caleb hedged, since he had indeed been digging.

Alan's expression made it clear that he wasn't buying it. "My wife and I have known her a lotta years, so yeah. We call her by her real name."

"Has she been headlining here long?"

"A while. When she moved back a few years ago, she was desperate for a second job, something to keep her from going stir-crazy after sunset, she said. I think she was more of a mind to serve drinks, but we'd just lost our regular act, and she thought it would be fun to fill in till we got someone new. She's still filling in."

Filling in as a second job. Meaning her day job left her evenings free. Caleb wondered how big a town Mistletoe actually was, and if he made a trip down the mountain, how long it would take him to stroll the main streets and find her?

And then he thought back to the rest of what Alan had said. That a few years ago Candy had moved back. From where? "She said her only previous singing experience was with a church choir."

"Yeah. That was hard to believe when she got up onstage the first time. It was like she was born to perform."

"Whose idea was the costume?"

"Both of ours. She wanted to keep her two lives separate, and I wanted something to fit with the theme of the inn."

Candy Cane. Club Crimson. One in Vermillion. Will Ruby Mine. And the theme didn't stop at the color red. Just this morning when at the front desk convincing registration to let him stay the weekend, he'd seen a delivery from a shop called Under the Mistletoe.

He wouldn't be surprised to find Santa living in town. "She said your wife wanted her to sing at some school dance."

"She does, but it's not going to happen, which is fine. There's a girl in town who's going to perform. Zoe Sparks. She's amazing."

Brenna's sister sang? Caleb wondered how her mother felt about that, and if meeting the girl might answer his question about their estrangement. Then he wondered if Brenna's family even had a clue about the wedding. He picked up his glass, swirling the ice in the water. A trip into town might be in order after all. He'd have to hire a car…

"Lights are going down. Do you want anything else before the show starts?"

Already? He'd been so lost in thought he hadn't noticed the music he was now hearing was the pianist who'd taken the stage to warm up.

"No, I'm good," he told Alan, realizing the time he'd spent talking to the bartender was the time he was supposed to be getting a better handle on Candy by taking in the place where she worked, the mood of those who came to see her.

Alan had given him some of that, but Caleb was suddenly struck with the urge to go. This wasn't where or how he wanted to see her again. He didn't want to share her with the bartender, with the pianist or with the crowd.

When he was with her again, he wanted it to be just the two of them. Sitting and listening to her sing, watching her as she strolled through the club flirting and touching was more than he could handle. After what they'd shared last night, the thought of her being so close without having her…he couldn't do it. He couldn't stay.

He patted his jacket pocket, found a pen and his notepad, then scrambled for a way to leave her a note that no one at the bar could open and read. "Hey, Alan, you wouldn't happen to have an envelope, would you?"

"An envelope?" Alan walked the length of the bar, digging through drawers and stacks of papers near the register. He came back a moment later with a window envelope meant for bill payments. "Will this work?"

"Sure, thanks." Caleb jotted his note to Candy whoever-she-was, slipped that along with his room key inside, and considered adding a condom, but thought better of taking his invitation that far.

He scratched her first name across the back, drew a cane for her last, smiled at the sap he was for falling for the schmaltz. He waved Alan to come back. "Can you give this to her after the show?"

"You're not sticking around?" the bartender asked, taking the envelope from Caleb's hand and studying it as if he could see through the paper to the contents.

"Can't. Something's come up." Caleb boosted himself off

the stool, then hurried out before Alan asked for details and he had to lie. "Just see that Candy gets the note."

As SHE DID EVERY NIGHT following her show, Miranda—still decked out as Candy—climbed onto a bar stool to unwind while Alan closed up the club. Unlike every other night following her show, she didn't see much unwinding ahead.

She'd poured out her heart tonight, had lost herself in the lyrics as she'd sung. It had been hard to wait for just the right moment to step off the stage and walk into the crowd.

Too soon, and the audience wouldn't be receptive. Too late, and they'd be anxious to get back to their rooms with their lovers. Strange that she'd waited till her final song last night. She never waited that long.

What had been different? Why the blip in her routine? She didn't want to think what she would've missed out on had she not changed things up.

But that was then. Tonight was tonight. She'd tried not to think of Caleb while singing, but it was hard to separate the emotions inspired by the love songs from the spiral of feelings she'd been riding all day. She didn't love him; of course she didn't love him, but the high of lust and infatuation was undeniable.

What she couldn't understand was why he hadn't been there to hear her. And then to return to the club and find out that he hadn't even come downstairs to meet her after the show? "I want the largest appletini you can make. And then I want another."

Alan started in mixing the drink. "How 'bout you finish one before I waste the makings of a second?"

Oh, yeah? "Just because I was stood up, you think I can't handle two drinks?"

"You weren't stood up," he said, adding apple schnapps to the vodka, apple juice and Cointreau. "Not exactly."

She whipped her head around to search the club. It was empty. Even the back booth where Caleb had sat last night. "What do you mean? What are you saying?"

He reached into the pocket of his apron, pulled out an envelope with her name written across the back, waved it at her like a flag. "He left you a note."

"Caleb?" Caleb had left her a note? And Alan thought he was going to play keep-away? This was so not funny.

"Were you hoping for one from someone else?"

"Well, give it to me already," she said, her heart pounding as she leaned across the bar and snatched it, tucking it into her cleavage for safekeeping.

Her ex-friend laughed like a hyena as he poured her drink into a large martini glass and handed it to her. "Who knew we were still in high school?"

"I think I'd prefer to read my note in private, thank you very much," she said, swiveling her stool away from the bar, her hand holding the drink in the air as she eased down.

"Hey! No taking drinks out of the club," Alan called from behind her as she wound her way through the tables, sofas and chairs toward the stage.

"Call the manager," she tossed back, climbing the steps and making her way to the rear exit. "Tell him I'll be in my dressing room."

She couldn't get there fast enough. The envelope was itching and scratching and tearing at her skin. It wasn't really, she knew. It was her anxiety, her wanting to know what Caleb had said, what excuse he'd made, if he'd left the Inn at Snow Falls and Mistletoe without a word of goodbye except for what she held in her hand.

She dropped to her bench, swallowed a quarter of her drink before setting it on her vanity, and caught her reflection in the mirror when she did. Makeup aside, her cheeks were flushed, her neck, too, the high color an outward display of the rush of blood through her veins.

Why was she letting Caleb leaving her a note get to her? They did not have a relationship. They'd met twenty-four hours ago, and could barely call themselves friends. Yes, he had told her that he would come to the show tonight, that he'd be prepared to finish what they'd started last night.

He could've changed his mind, gotten a better offer, been called away on business, gone to bed early with the fever and cough he'd come down with after she'd forced him out into the snow. But holding the envelope with a shaking hand while staring at her reflection and borrowing mental trouble was not going to fill in the blanks.

She reached for her glass, took another big gulp, then slid a finger beneath the envelope's flap. Inside she found a sheet torn from a pocket-size notebook and a room key.

Miranda held the key, her heart racing, her head pounding, her stomach tossing and turning. And then she unfolded the paper and read the single word Caleb had written.

Come

# 10

HEADING BACK TO HIS ROOM to wait for Candy hadn't been the best idea after all. Caleb swore he'd paced a trough to China during her set. At the end of the hour following her set, when the knock on his door finally came, he twitched hard enough to snap his spine.

He'd given her a key; was it somebody else outside? Had she come to return it instead of use it? Could he be any more relieved that he hadn't been a jerk and included a condom with the key and the note?

He glanced around the room, made sure nothing of Max had been left out, then went to answer. He didn't even bother with the peephole. If it wasn't Candy whoever-she-was, well, he wanted the surprise either way.

He pulled open the door to find her standing there wearing her sheepskin boots, his blazer from last night, her wig and the long slinky gown she'd obviously performed in. She had her parka draped over one arm. In her other hand, she clutched the handles of the same red gym bag she'd been carrying when he'd followed her through the kitchen.

He didn't want to try to interpret the expression on her face. She wasn't smiling or frowning. He couldn't tell if she was calm or scared stiff. All he knew was that if she stayed out in the hallway, he wasn't going to find out any of what she was thinking.

Holding open the door, he stepped back to give her room to enter. She took a deep breath, and did. He let the door close, and saw her jump when the latch caught and clicked.

She was nervous. He was nervous.

Whether they slept together or not, they needed to get nervous out of the way.

He walked up behind her, cleared his throat so she'd know he was there, took her parka and her bag from her hands. He tossed the small duffel to the floor of the closet and hung up the coat next to his.

She turned then, shrugged out of the blazer he'd left her wearing last night, and held it out in offering.

He waited, staring, knowing they had to break this ice or the night—whether they had sex or stuck to conversation— was going to be a disaster. When he saw the corner of her mouth quirk and one brow begin to lift, he moved.

His chest tight, he took the jacket, tossed it to the floor, held her face between his hands and kissed her.

She clutched his biceps and whimpered, leaning into him and parting her lips. His heart beat like a hammer as he slanted his mouth over hers and groaned, breathing her in, tasting her, wanting so much more of her than he could get with the two of them still fully clothed.

It was Candy and what she wanted that kept him from pushing things further. He was ready for anything, ready for it now, but he sensed that for her it was too soon. That she had things she needed to settle, things she needed to say.

He was right.

She eased her grip on his arms, pulling her mouth from his and backing away. A shy smile crossed her face. "You know I can't think when you do that."

"Guess that means I'm doing it right."

"Oh, you're doing it right," she said, laughing softly. Then she took another step away and wrapped her arms around herself. "Aren't you wondering why I didn't use the key?"

He moved his hands to his hips. "I am, but I figured if you wanted me to know, you'd tell me."

"Honestly? I'm not sure me being here is a good idea."

Right now, he couldn't think of a better one unless it was the two of them getting naked. "And you thought if I didn't answer you'd be off the hook?"

"No. Nothing like that."

"Then why did you come?" he asked, confused.

"Because I want to be here."

"You want to be here. You're just not sure it's a good idea. Got it." Yeah, this was going well.

"I had the best time with you last night. The dressing room. Sneaking into the kitchen. Your goodnight kiss. And condom or not, if you had pushed, I wouldn't have said no," she said, and he saw color bloom on her cheeks.

If he'd only known that then, he mused with no small amount of sarcasm, before admitting to himself that he had known it. That he'd had to force himself to walk away and leave her at her dressing-room door.

He scrubbed a hand down his jaw. "Look, Candy—"

"It's Miranda."

"What?" Stunned, he whipped his gaze up to meet hers.

She took a deep breath and rushed out with it again. "My name is Miranda. And that's why I'm not sure being here is a good idea."

That didn't make any sense. "Because your name is Miranda?"

"No," she said, her voice soft, patient. "Because I can't be with you as Candy. And being with you as myself is not an easy thing for me to do."

Once she got out of her clothes, he'd show her how easy it was. But he knew that was not what she meant.

"Okay…Miranda." He paused, searched for a new tack to take, since kissing her hadn't turned out to be such a brilliant idea. "Are you hungry? Should I order room service? Do you want a drink?" He sure as hell wanted one.

She shook her head. "No. All I want is you. To make love with you. But now that I've had time to think, I know that I can only do it as myself."

The drink could wait. "Does that mean you're going to tell me all of your secrets?"

"I don't think so," she said with a laugh. "Only my name, and this."

As Caleb looked on, she reached up and pulled off her wig. Her hair beneath was the short dark color he'd guessed from the strands caught in the bristles of her brush. Or so he first thought.

When she reached up to fluff it, pinching her bangs into wisps and shaking the rest of the layers, he realized it was more red than brown.

"You really are a redhead."

"Of a sort," she said, and blushed.

"Do you have freckles on your nose?" he asked, tickled by this whole discovery process.

"My nose, my cheeks. My forehead. And if you'll give me five minutes to wash off my makeup, I'll let you see for yourself."

He was all over seeing for himself. He didn't say a word, just gestured toward the bathroom and bowed. She walked by him and shoved his shoulder, knocking him back to the bed.

He laughed, but he didn't look away, only propped himself

up on his elbows far enough to see her grab his jacket from where he'd tossed it before closing the bathroom door.

He lay there for several moments, listening to the water run, then jumped up and got rid of his shoes, socks and shirt, keeping his pants on for now. He turned off the light nearest the bed, leaving on the one nearest the window, then sat down in one of the room's two wing chairs to wait.

He was still sitting there, leaning forward and staring at the floor, his elbows on his knees, his hands laced and his head hanging, when the water stopped, the bathroom door opened and Miranda came out.

He didn't care about her last name. He didn't care about her secrets. He didn't care that everything up until now had been awkward, tense and the bad idea she'd suggested. All he cared about was getting her clothes off and showing her with his body all the things he was feeling but was too tongue-tied to say.

She stood at the edge of the bedroom, the light of the bathroom behind her, seeming almost uncertain, hesitant, as if she needed his approval before taking another step. If he could've found his voice in that moment, he would've have given it a thousand times over. His voice, his heart, his brain...none of it was working.

He was looking at the most amazing creature he'd ever seen in his life. As Candy, she was gorgeous, classy, seductive. As Miranda...words failed him—a sad state for someone who made his living using them. But this wasn't gossip or a story for the hungry hordes. This was the two of them acting on an attraction that had him struggling to make sense of blindsiding emotion.

She was naked except for her panties and his blazer. Her face was scrubbed clean, her hair fluffed in layers and bangs. The lapels of the coat hung open, baring a long strip of skin from between her breasts to her sex that was covered by a triangle of white cotton. The look in her eyes was one of longing— and hope.

His hands on the chair arms, he pushed to his feet and walked toward her, slid his fingers beneath the jacket where it covered her shoulders and pushed it down her arms. It fell to the floor and left her standing in a scrap of a thong.

Running his hands down her arms, from her shoulders to her elbows, he tried to drink her all in, her green eyes, her freckles, her hair, still feeling a tug of familiarity but no longer trying to put his finger on the source. Right now? He didn't care.

She was here. She was beautiful. She was his.

Again, he struggled with words. "You are absolutely perfect, did you know that?"

"I'm absolutely terrified, does it show?"

He moved to her hands, found them shaking and held them. "I don't see anything but a long night ahead."

"I'm not too freckled? Too plain?" She looked down at herself. "Too small?"

She was talking about her breasts. She didn't have a lover, hadn't had one in how long? And she was worried he would find her breasts too small? Who had told her they were? Who had told her she was anything but incredible?

He brought up his hands to cup her, catching her nipples with his forefingers and thumbs, rolling the tight tips and leaning down to kiss the crease between her shoulder and her neck.

She sucked in a sharp breath, covered his hands with her own, guided him to touch her the way she wanted, shuddering when he did as if he'd given her the world.

"Good?" he asked, his mouth at her collarbone.

"Oh, yes. So good."

He wanted to make it even better, to show her what she'd been missing, and drifted lower, kissing his way down the slope of one breast, tugging at her nipple with his lips. She made tiny sounds in her throat, wiggled and squirmed, threaded her fingers into his hair and pulled.

He looked up, met her gaze, ran the tip of his tongue around the tip of her breast while she watched. Her eyes grew smoky and wicked hot, she bit at her lower lip, slowly shook her head and said, "Let's go to bed."

The bed, the floor, up against the wall, the chair and the desk...anywhere was fine with him as long as he could have her. And knowing she wanted him, too? He was afraid this first time would be over as fast as it started, but there was nothing he could do.

He stood, began to wrap her in his arms and tumble them both to the mattress, but stopped. He wanted her out of her panties.

He didn't ask. Just pushed his hands beneath the strip of elastic that held them in place and shoved them to her feet. He remembered touching her last night, how smooth she was, how wet on his fingers. He wanted to know that she was just as ready for him now.

She stepped out of the fabric and reached for his fly, unbuckling, unbuttoning, unzipping while he slid a finger into her folds, separating the plump lips of her pussy, finding her clit hard and bold.

And then her hands were holding him, the sac of his balls, his rigid shaft, lifting him out of his shorts then letting him go while she pulled his pants down. That was when he finally tumbled her, grabbing her up and falling with her to the bed.

She giggled as if she couldn't imagine having more fun, and he found himself smiling, too, loving the foreplay because of the joy reflected in her face. But he could only stand the teasing touches of her fingers and her mouth so long. Enough had become enough.

He pinned her down and moved on top of her, rose up to his knees and rolled on a condom while she watched. Her eyes were hungry, and he hurried, bracing his hands above her shoulders while she guided him into place.

He surged forward, driving into her. She gasped, thrust upward, settled back onto the mattress and closed her legs around his hips, her arms around his back.

She pulled him down, and he lowered his weight to his elbows, riding her, rocking against her, filling her with every slow, smooth stroke. He wanted to take hours, knew they only had minutes. The heat of this connection was a fiery one, consuming them.

She took him in, clenched her muscles and held him, grinding hard. He wanted her to stop, to be still, to let him go. This was happening too fast. He wasn't going to be able to hold on. He needed to know she was getting what she wanted, that he wasn't letting her down. But he couldn't wait, he couldn't wait. He had too much need.

"I can't—" he started to say, then lost the words in his throat.

"It's okay," she told him, breathless, her voice breaking. "I can't either."

He closed his eyes and gave up his control, spilling himself as she ground her sex to his shaft and cried out. He came quickly, fiercely, felt her spasms at the same time. The sensations rocked him physically, but a strange pulse of emotion followed.

He didn't want to deal with it now, but he couldn't push it away. His body was still humming, his desire still winding down. So he allowed the sense of rightness to wash over him as he pulled out of her body and spooned close to her side.

She cuddled back against him, but only stayed a minute or two before excusing herself and heading to the bathroom. He discarded the condom in the room's wastebasket, listening to the water running, the toilet flushing, and realized how intimate it was hearing Miranda clean up after sex.

Miranda—and, yeah, he liked that name so much better than Candy—opened the bathroom door, switched off the light, and wearing nothing but her skin, crawled beneath the covers and rested her head on his shoulder. He was surprised at how perfect it felt to have her there, how comfortable he was holding her close.

"You staying the night?" he finally asked.

"I can. Most of it anyway. Unless you want me to go."

"Hell, no. I'd like to get in a round two and three at least." Rounds during which they would take their time exploring instead of exploding. He wanted to know what it was he was feeling with her, why he was feeling anything at all.

She tugged at the hair on his chest. "Awful full of yourself, aren't you?"

"I'd rather you be full of me."

"I'd like that. Maybe a marathon this time instead of a sprint?"

Ouch. "Hey. Who're you calling a sprinter?"

She rolled toward him, rose over him on one elbow. "The man who sprinted?"

He crossed his arms beneath his head on his pillow. "I'm pretty sure that race was a photo finish."

"I like a photo finish. It's exciting. Especially after a marathon."

A one-track mind, this woman with the freckles on her nose. "How 'bout I lie back here and give you a head start?"

"Wouldn't that be giving you the head start?"

"If you want to get technical…"

But that was all he got out before she climbed on top and straddled him. His cock stood at attention against her belly, and it was the biggest fight of his life to keep his hands beneath his head. He wanted to pull her down, press her breasts together, tongue his way from one nipple to the other and make her squirm.

Instead, he closed his eyes and let her play, lying as still as he could as she started at his collarbone, moved to the dip in his throat, kissing and licking her way down his chest, to his belly, to his cock.

She kissed the full head, flicked the tip of her tongue over the slit, had him muttering silent curses when she wrapped her lips around him and sucked.

She ringed her fingers at the top of his shaft, stroked them up and down his glans as she pulled at him with her mouth. His balls drew up tight against his body, and it took everything he had in him not to come.

But everything wasn't enough. He tried to warn her, reaching down to pull out, but she shook her head, pushed his hand away, and sucked him harder and faster until he bucked his hips and came.

She took all of him, stayed right there with him, only letting him go when he groaned to let her know he was done. *Done* wasn't even the half of it. He was spent, exhausted. He wanted nothing more than to sprawl across the bed and sleep.

He'd promised her a marathon, however, so he flipped her to her back, knelt between her spread legs, and with a rumbling growl as he went down on her, said, "My turn."

# *11*

MIRANDA'S INTERNAL CLOCK went off before her cell-phone alarm could ring and wake Caleb. She rolled away from him as quietly as she could, realizing as she stretched that Patrice's predictions had come true.

Her muscles were all kinds of sore, her skin rubbed raw and bruised, and if she managed to get out of bed in one piece, she would definitely be hobbling like an old woman all the way to her car.

She had no idea what had happened to the thong she'd been wearing, and couldn't worry about that now. Instead, she crept to the closet and found her gym bag. Tugging gingerly on the zipper pull, she opened the duffel and dug through her things for panties, socks and a bra.

After reading the note, no, the *word* Caleb had left for her last night, the only thing she'd wanted to know was why he hadn't come to her show. The more she thought about it, however, the more she appreciated his not being there.

Looking for him in the crowd had been distracting enough. She couldn't imagine the distraction if she'd found him. Maybe he'd anticipated that and stayed away to save her performance from swirling down the tubes.

She'd meant to ask him about it when he'd opened the door. She hadn't meant to seize up with nerves and forget everything except telling him her name.

But he'd stood there staring at her, looking all disheveled and unhinged as if the wait had been driving him mad, and her long list of questions had dissolved into nothing but wanting to hear him call her Miranda.

She should be glad she'd managed to do that much, she mused, tugging on her socks before digging for her sweatshirt and pulling it over her head. The rest of the answers she wanted could wait. She figured he had a few things on his mind, too. Funny how nothing else had mattered to either of them when faced with a marathon of sex.

She was just starting to pull on her thermal bottoms and sweatpants when the light beside the bed clicked on. She cringed, stepped forward, peered around the corner to see Caleb propped up on his elbows, frowning as if looking for what woke him.

"Sorry," she whispered. "I was trying to be quiet."

"You *were* quiet." He sat up, scrubbing his hands over his face. The sheet fell to his lap and left her looking at the chest that she'd come to know so well, the hair in the center that was silky and soft. "I got cold. Where are you going?"

"Home." He was gorgeous, all warm and sleepy-looking. She didn't want to go. "I have work, remember?"

That sobered him. He tossed the sheet out of the way and wearing absolutely nothing but the stirrings of a hard-on, walked toward her. He didn't smile or speak or give her a chance to catch up. He just backed her into the wall and brought his mouth down on hers.

Oh, this was so not fair, this way he caused her to forget everything but his body and what it could do, the magic he could make her feel. She had not had this in so long—if she'd had it ever. He'd taken her over so completely, she couldn't remember any other men at all.

He held her shoulders, kissed his way from her mouth to her ear then down her neck to her sweatshirt. He stopped there, grunted, reached for the hem and pushed the fabric up over her breasts. He grunted again at finding her wearing a bra, but the garment didn't stop him from sucking her nipple into his mouth.

She threaded her fingers into his hair. "I've got to go."

"I've got to come."

She laughed. "Again? I can't believe you have anything left in you."

"A machine, baby. I am a machine."

She tugged up his head, forced him to look at her. "I have one of those at home. It's called a vibrator."

"Sorry. Half asleep. Not thinking with my big head."

Being a man, in other words. "You go back to bed. I'm going home."

"Why don't you come back to bed with me, then I'll go home with you?"

She closed her eyes, moaned in pleasure as he pinched both nipples, tugging and rolling them while sucking on the skin at the base of her neck. It was a good thing she had more than one costume with a banded collar neckline. She was going to have bruises to hide.

And then she remembered it was Thursday. Tonight was her night off. The thought of not seeing him… "Why don't I go home now, and you come later? For dinner."

He stopped with his hands only halfway into her panties. Then pulled them out, and looked up. "You want me to come to your house? Like, Miranda's house, not Candy's house?"

She cocked her head to the side. "Candy doesn't have a house. She has a dressing room."

He frowned. "I didn't think you wanted me to know who you are."

"Not all of it. Not yet." She paused, considered everything she knew about him, considered all the things she still didn't. "You scare me."

"Really? I didn't think my cock was that big."

It was hard to keep a straight face. "Please. Not that kind of scared. Though if I don't get away from you, I am afraid I'll never walk without hobbling again."

He scratched his chest, his grin all cock-of-the-walk proud.

She pushed him away, fighting an answering smile. "Move so I can get my pants on."

"You look a lot better with them off."

"That's because you're looking with your southernmost eye." She didn't even want to think about how good he looked out of his clothes or she'd never get to the shop in time to avoid a scolding from Corinne.

He leaned a hand on the wall next to her head, whispering into her ear as he nibbled her lobe, moved down to the skin of her neck, "What time do you want me to come?"

She was not going to play this game of double entendre. She was not. It didn't matter that just the right touch and she'd melt all over him.

Since she was usually home from the shop by six... "Eight?"

"Where do you want me to come?" he asked, nuzzling her neck.

She was not, she was not, she was not going to play. She ducked out from under his arm, shoved her feet into her Uggs and grabbed her parka and duffel from the closet. "Second Avenue. Twelve-oh-five."

"Miranda?"

She turned back. The way he said her name... She wanted to weep from the beauty of hearing it. Her heart thundered in her chest. "Yes?"

"After dinner, can I come? Can I make you come? Can we have another photo-finish marathon of coming? Or take turns all night long?"

As if she could turn down a man who begged as beautifully as he made love. "After dinner, you can come until the machine won't come anymore."

"TEN-THIRTY YESTERDAY. Eleven today. By next week you'll be showing up at closing time."

"I know, I know. I'm sorry." Miranda stashed her purse in her locker, pulled on her apron, wondered if she'd remembered to brush her hair. She hadn't bothered with more than mascara, running as late as she was. "I spent the night at the inn. I forgot how long it can take to get down the mountain with the sun glaring off the snow."

"You spent the night at the inn? With him?"

"That's not all."

One of Corinne's brows went up. "You told him who you were."

"Only my first name," Miranda said, holding up one finger. "But I did invite him for dinner tonight."

Clucking like a hen, Corinne went back to work. "When all of this blows up in your face, I don't want to hear about it. You've got too many secrets to make a relationship work, unless you're planning to come clean."

An understatement if Miranda had ever heard one. "Right now, it's just sex. It's not a relationship. There's nothing to blow up or any need to come clean."

"Tell yourself that now," the other woman said, using a pair of scissors as a pointer. "And I'll remind you of it later when you realize you're over your head and drowning."

Knowing the subject of relationships was a touchy one for

Corinne, who'd been alone years longer than she had, Miranda switched to something a little more pressing. "What should I make for dinner?"

"What does he like?"

They hadn't exactly gotten around to sharing their favorite foods. "I have no idea. I don't know if he's a vegetarian or a vegan, or a meat-and-potatoes guy."

"Meatless lasagna, salad and bread sticks," Corinne suggested.

Easy enough, but… "What if he doesn't like veggies? Or what if he's allergic to wheat?"

Still brandishing the scissors, Corinne turned to face her. "Why don't you call him and ask?"

"Now that's an idea," Miranda said, heading for the phone. She dialed the switchboard at the inn, booting up her laptop while waiting for the operator to answer. "Room two-eighteen please."

Muttering to herself, Corinne got back to cutting stems from filler carnations.

"McGregor," Caleb said, picking up after four rings.

Hearing his voice brought back all of last night in a mental slideshow. Miranda tucked the phone close to her chin, feeling her cheeks flush. "Caleb? Miranda. Are you a vegetarian? Do you have any food allergies? Is there anything you won't eat? Broccoli or bacon or béchamel sauce?"

He laughed, the sound echoing richly through the line. "If I knew what that was, I might turn up my nose, but I'm good with grilled cheese or a PB and J."

"I'm not going to feed you a PB and J, but I don't want to feed you shrimp if you're going to break out in hives."

"No hives. No worries. But while I have you…what're you wearing?"

"Goodbye, Caleb," she said, and hung up before he could respond. Fanning her face with one hand, she turned to Corinne. "We're good to go with anything."

"What's this *we* business? You're the one jumping from the frying pan into the fire. Though judging by your face, I'd say you already made the leap."

She'd made some kind of leap. She just hadn't yet figured out where she'd landed. In a relationship or in a fling? Back to the food. "Italian?"

"Too much garlic," Corinne said sagely.

"Steaks and stuffed baked potatoes?"

"If you want to be the ones stuffed." Again, more sound advice.

"I want to make a good first impression," Miranda said, humbled by the fact that she, who had worked with caterers on events feeding hundreds of strangers, couldn't decide what to cook for a man she'd spent a very long passionate night getting to know.

Corinne snorted. "If the burn marks on your jaw are any indication, I'd say you've moved beyond first, to a second or third at least."

Crap. Miranda headed for the bathroom and peered at her reflection in the mirror above the sink. She turned her head left, then right, finding a spot scraped red by Caleb's whiskers.

She hadn't bothered with foundation this morning, already in a hurry to get to the shop, and obviously she should have. Good thing she kept a bag of makeup samples in her locker.

She was covering the red marks when Corinne appeared in the doorway behind her. "Make it simple."

Miranda froze with her hand halfway to her face. "I was only using foundation."

Corinne shook her head. "Not your makeup. Dinner. Stuff

some chicken breasts. I've got a great recipe using spinach and goat cheese. Or forget stuffing. That's not exactly simple. Just bake. If he turns out to be handy in the kitchen, put him in charge of a salad, or at least the wine. You can talk while all the prep is going on, get to know him better. He could be the one, and I don't need to be putting an old-hag damper on things."

"You're not putting a damper on things," Miranda said, frowning as she turned away from the mirror to look at her friend. "Why would you even think that?"

Standing just inside the bathroom, Corinne closed her eyes and dropped her head against the door. "Because I've been such a grump these past few days."

"Oh, Corinne. Being a grump does not make you an old hag," Miranda said, laying a hand on the other woman's arm, sensing the source of her unusual show of emotions. It couldn't be easy working on flowers that were more than likely for her own daughter's wedding. "We're all allowed to be grumpy from time to time. And some of those times can be really, really hard."

Corinne opened watery eyes and met Miranda's gaze. "I shouldn't have given away all the gifts Brenna sent. I've been so angry with her for so long. But giving away the things she sent was just cruel. I never meant to hurt her feelings."

"Of course you didn't," Miranda said, turning and drawing her friend into a hug. "And being cruel wasn't your intent. You were hurt—"

"Which is why I should've kept the gifts." Corinne pulled away. "I wasn't thinking straight."

With Corinne's guard down and her regret running high, Miranda decided to give her employee a push in the direction she was certain Corinne was ready to go. "You could always call the inn and talk to her."

Corinne stopped in the act of running her fingers beneath her eyes. "Apologize?"

"Not apologize. Explain. Open a dialogue."

"I don't know. I don't want to make things worse."

"Then think about calling her." Miranda was not giving up. "Thinking's harmless enough, isn't it?"

Corinne shrugged. "I guess if you can invite a stranger home and cook him dinner, I can think about settling things with my daughter."

## 12

---

BARRY CHANCE, the Inn at Snow Falls' shuttle driver, seemed to think Caleb was a tourist wanting a rundown on the resort and the town, when the only thing he wanted was to get to 1205 Second Avenue at eight o'clock on the nose.

From behind the wheel of the minivan warmed to near suffocation, Barry prattled on. "Twelve-oh-five Second Avenue. Isn't that Miranda Kelly's house?"

Miranda Kelly. Caleb stared out the side window into the darkness made even darker by the shadows cast by the thick evergreen forest on either side of the road.

*Miranda Kelly.* Nice, but not a name he could place in the context of freckles, green eyes and short auburn hair. Either he was thinking of someone else and he didn't know her at all, or she'd changed both her name and her looks.

He settled back, bracing his arm across the seat. "You know her then?"

"Everyone in Mistletoe knows Miranda. But then everyone in Mistletoe knows everyone in Mistletoe." That tickled the driver, and he cackled like a witch throwing newts' eyes into a cauldron. "She owns Under the Mistletoe, the flower shop. But then you probably know that, being friends with her and all."

"Sure," Caleb said as if affirming Barry's assumption,

wondering what else the other man knew and might share without Caleb having to dig.

"Corinne Sparks works there with her." Barry caught Caleb's gaze in the rearview mirror. "Her daughter Brenna's that singer Ravyn Black, though you probably know that, too. She's up at the inn. So's Congressman Eagleton."

Caleb figured he knew more about Teddy and the rock star than Barry did. But the rest was interesting. The sister at the high school. The mother at the flower shop. Maybe he could get to the secret of Brenna's family estrangement through Miranda.

Miranda Kelly. Nope. He didn't know the name.

"Here we are," the driver announced moments later, pointing out a tiny bungalow that sat back from the road, its long front walk and driveway shoveled, its yard a blanket of snow. "Do you need me to come back for you later?"

Caleb glanced through the windshield toward the light diffused by the front window's curtains. No way was he going to share his plans to stay the night with this gossip. "If Miranda doesn't want to drive me back, I'll call the inn."

Barry flung his arm along the seat, turning to look at Caleb sitting behind him. "I get off at midnight, so don't wait till the last minute or you'll be stuck here all night."

That was the idea.

"Thanks for the ride," Caleb said, climbing out into the street and waving as the minivan pulled away. He made his way to the end of the walk that led to her house, studying the small Craftsman structure, the smoke rising from the chimney, the welcoming glow of the porch lamp.

Heading up the front walk, he imagined her inside, all warm and cozy as she fussed with dishes and food, setting the table, lighting candles, arranging flowers she'd brought home from her shop. And then he wondered what the hell he'd

## The Harlequin Reader Service — Here's how it works:

Accepting your 2 free books and 2 free mystery gifts places you under no obligation to buy anything. You may keep the books and gifts and return the shipping statement marked "cancel". If you do not cancel, about a month later we'll send you 6 additional books and bill you just $4.24 each in the U.S. or $4.71 each in Canada. That is a savings of at least 15% off the cover price. It's quite a bargain! Shipping and handling is just 25¢ per book, along with any applicable taxes.* You may cancel at any time, but if you choose to continue, every month we'll send you 6 more books, which you may either purchase at the discount price or return to us and cancel your subscription.

*Terms and prices subject to change without notice. Sales tax applicable in N.Y. Canadian residents will be charged applicable provincial taxes and GST. Offer not valid in Quebec. All orders subject to approval. Credit or debit balances in a customer's account(s) may be offset by any other outstanding balance owed by or to the customer. Please allow 4 to 6 weeks for delivery. Offer available while quantities last.

NO POSTAGE
NECESSARY
IF MAILED
IN THE
UNITED STATES

**BUSINESS REPLY MAIL**

FIRST-CLASS MAIL     PERMIT NO. 717     BUFFALO, NY

POSTAGE WILL BE PAID BY ADDRESSEE

HARLEQUIN READER SERVICE
3010 WALDEN AVE
PO BOX 1867
BUFFALO NY 14240-9952

If offer card is missing write to: The Harlequin Reader Service, 3010 Walden Ave., P.O. Box 1867, Buffalo, NY 14240-1867

# Do You Have the LUCKY KEY?

## PLAY THE Lucky Key Game
### and you can get

# FREE BOOKS and FREE GIFTS!

*Scratch the gold areas with a coin. Then check below to see the books and gifts you can get!*

## YES! I have scratched off the gold areas. Please send me the 2 FREE BOOKS and 2 FREE GIFTS, worth about $10, for which I qualify. I understand I am under no obligation to purchase any books, as explained on the back of this card.

**351 HDL EVLT**                    **151 HDL EVP5**

FIRST NAME                    LAST NAME

ADDRESS

APT.#        CITY

STATE/PROV.        ZIP/POSTAL CODE

**www.eHarlequin.com**

2 free books plus 2 free gifts

1 free book

2 free books

Try Again!

DETACH AND MAIL CARD TODAY!

(H-B-11/08)

© 2008 HARLEQUIN ENTERPRISES LIMITED. ® and ™ trademarks owned and used by the trademark owner and/or its licensee.

been smoking, painting that domestic scene, and ignored the strange aching tug in his chest as he rang the bell and waited for her to answer.

She pulled open the door moments later, a flurry of sounds and scents coming with her, her eyes going wide when she saw that he was wearing only a blazer with his dress shirt and jeans, and had his sheepskin coat in one hand.

"Aren't you freezing?"

"Only marginally," he said, and when she didn't invite him in, added with a forced chatter of teeth, "Though the longer I stay out here, the worse it gets."

"Oh, geez. Sorry. Come in." She stepped back, let him pass, then closed the door, taking his coat and hanging it in the front room's closet. "I was so busy ogling you, I forgot my manners, *oomph*—"

He crushed her to him, his mouth coming down to cover hers in a punishing kiss, though he didn't know who he was punishing. Himself for being so besotted with her, or her for besotting him the way she had.

And then it didn't matter because she was kissing him back, her hands on his shoulders, her tongue in his mouth, her legs wound up with his, her breasts pressed to his chest. He groaned. She groaned. She whimpered and squirmed and then shoved him away.

"Dinner first," she told him breathlessly, her eyes sparkling with the heat of the kiss as the fire leaped in the fireplace behind her.

"What if I want to skip dinner and go straight for dessert?" he asked her, his chest rising and falling as he fought back his desire.

"Then you can follow me into the kitchen and have a slice of Italian cream cake while I finish stuffing the chicken breasts." And with that, she turned, not looking back to see if he was coming with her.

He didn't have much choice, and cake sounded good, so he followed.

"I didn't think you were really going to cook," he said, climbing onto a stool on the other side of the center island from where she worked. "I thought it was all a big pretense to get me in bed."

"You may live on sex and grilled cheese," she said, grabbing a small plate and a cake knife. "But I like a more balanced diet."

He looked at the colorful array of food laid out, inhaling herbs and spices and something...sharp. "Veggies, protein, sex and sugar?"

"Plus singing, working and spending time with friends."

"So I'm a friend, huh?" he asked, grabbing a wedge of bell pepper and popping it into his mouth. He crunched down, felt the tang and the crispness, and reached for another.

Miranda set the cake plate aside and offered him the handle of the small paring knife that had been lying on the island. "You're welcome to work on the salad."

He took it with a teasing grumble. "Not only do I have to wait for sex, now I have to work for my dinner."

She turned around, reached into her pantry, came back with a loaf of bread and jar of peanut butter, and set both in front of him. "I happen to think the best things are worth waiting for. If you don't, feel free to make a sandwich with your left hand, and use your right as you wish."

Oh, he liked this woman. "Saucy tonight, aren't we...Miranda Kelly?"

She froze in the act of mixing cooked spinach with chopped onions and some sort of pasty white cheese, and was slow to lift her gaze. "How did you find out my name? The Kelly part."

"The shuttle driver was a talker," he said, reaching for the salad bowl of lettuce and other greens and pretending not to notice the panic that flashed through her eyes.

"Did he tell you anything else?"

"He did, yes."

"Like what?"

"That you own a flower shop. That you employ the mother of Evermore's Ravyn Black. That he gets off work at midnight, and to call before that if I need a ride back." He added the last part because he was no longer sure that she'd want him to stay.

She didn't say anything at first, just got back to stirring and stuffing, arranging the chicken breasts in a shallow glass dish and putting them in to bake. Then she chose a bottle of wine from the small built-in rack above her refrigerator and set it on the island with two glasses.

"Barry's a sweetheart, but he does like to make conversation when he drives." She climbed onto the stool beside him, picked up a second paring knife.

Since she didn't stab him with it or ask him to leave, he figured so far so good. "Did you not want me knowing your last name? Or about Under the Mistletoe?"

"It's not that," she began, then shook her head. "That's not true. It is that. My life here is private, and I want to keep it that way."

The curiosity was killing him. "Miranda, I don't know who you are, so I don't know who I'd tell about you or the flower shop even if I was inclined to do so, which I'm not. So relax. Please." He reached for the wine bottle. "Now, did you want a drink? Or were you planning to bash me in the head with this and hope for amnesia?"

She gave him a weak smile, obviously still a bit hesitant to accept him at his word. "A drink would be nice, yes, thanks."

He poured a glass for both of them, watching her swallow half of hers before he'd taken his first sip. He didn't think his being here was making her nervous as much as his knowing her last name, and he found that extremely telling.

They both knew he could easily do an Internet search and most likely discover the story she was hiding. He supposed he could set her at ease by promising he wouldn't pry, but he'd already written a mental note to do just that when he got back to his laptop and the inn's wireless connection to the Web.

So he didn't say anything. He just waited, watching as she cut a red pepper and a yellow pepper to go with his green, deciding, when the silence lingered, to change the subject. "I'm surprised you can get all these vegetables so readily. The grocery store I saw in town looked like the small-canned-goods type."

"I cheated," she said, smiling. "I had Alan get them from the inn's kitchen. The goat cheese, too."

A big *eww* went though Caleb's head. "Goat cheese?"

Miranda chuckled. "Oh, don't be turning your nose up now, Mr. I'll-Eat-Anything. You had your chance to give me a list of food deemed off-limits."

"It wouldn't have occurred to me to mention it," he said, leaning away from the bowl with the leftover white lumps clinging to the glass. "I mean, is goat cheese a food?"

"Yes, it's a food, and you're going to eat it and love every bite."

He started to say something about eating her and loving her instead, but he had a feeling that discovering her name— no matter that he'd been given the information without asking—had sent him back to square one in the sex game.

Good thing he had Barry the shuttle driver's card. It was a hell of a long walk back to the inn. "Barry who likes to talk. He does know you're Candy Cane, right?"

"He does, yes."

"And Alan and his wife."

"Yes."

This time he went further. "Alan said he's known you a long time."

"He has," she admitted, her mouth quirking.

"Has anything bad happened with having them know about you being Candy?"

"No, but they're friends. They're not going to turn my dual identity into a human-interest story the way a reporter who got hold of the information might do," she said pointedly. "I don't want to risk having Candy's picture show up next to mine in the newspaper."

Because then someone who was looking for Miranda might see the article about her and Candy Cane, and boom. End of privacy. Now he wanted to know everything. "Who's looking for you, Miranda? Who are you hiding from?"

"What do you mean?" she asked, stalling, evading, clearly knowing exactly what he meant but obviously hoping to throw him off track. "All I said was that I didn't want my picture in the paper next to one of Candy."

Fine. She wanted him to spell it out? He'd spell it out. "People who know you wouldn't need the side-by-side pictures. They'd recognize you just from your name and identity as a florist. That means there's someone else out there you don't want making the connection."

She waved him off, reaching for extra spinach leaves that she hadn't cooked for the chicken. "You're thinking about this way too hard."

"Am I?" he asked, not easily dismissed.

"Yes. I'll take back what I said about the pictures, okay? If that'll quell your suspicions? I don't want my name linked to Candy's by some reporter wanting to write an article on her or Mistletoe. I like my privacy. Is that better?"

Better for her, maybe.

He shifted on his stool, reached for the wine and refilled both their glasses. "But outside of Mistletoe and the resort, who would care? Unless you're notorious in some way…"

"I'm not notorious," she said, her words tinged with a touch of desperation. She held up one hand. "I had a bad experience with the press and I don't want to relive it, okay?"

"Is there a reason you would have to?"

She set down the knife, and used the stem to slide her wineglass closer, but didn't drink, gathering her thoughts without ever glancing toward him. "Are there any reporters actively looking for me? I don't know. Are there reporters who would jump all over the news of me being here?" She nodded.

"The ones you had the bad experience with?"

"Yes. And it's those reporters I don't want seeing my picture or my name next to Candy's in the news. Satisfied?"

He should've been, but satisfaction wasn't what he was feeling. He was feeling that hunch again, the one telling him this story was big. "You know all I have to do is plug your name into Google and click go."

"I do. I'm just hoping you won't." The timer on the oven dinged. Saved by the bell, she jumped from her stool to pull the chicken from the oven. "Now. Let's eat."

# 13

Dinner was a very quiet affair. They ate at the small table in the alcove off Miranda's kitchen. The bungalow didn't have a formal dining room, so the entertaining she did was always as casual as tonight—though the menu was usually much simpler.

Parties of drinks and hors d'oeuvres for the holidays. Burgers on the backyard grill in the summer. Big kettles of soups and stews with bread from the inn's kitchen the rest of the year. A casserole shared with Corinne.

They had bread from the inn's kitchen tonight, too. A crusty artisan loaf that she served with a crock of real butter alongside their salad and stuffed chicken. The wine flowed freely. Very freely. More freely than was wise considering the conversation they'd had before sitting down to eat.

If she wasn't careful, she was going to spill everything about her past to Caleb just to get it off her chest. And because for some reason she didn't understand, she wanted him to know. She was obviously running on alcohol and hormones, but she got the feeling his curiosity was born of caring more than prurient nosiness.

His questions about her past showed his interest, and it felt so good to have that attention from a man. She knew he wouldn't be here long, making a relationship between them highly unlikely. Yet a part of her was unwilling to discount the possibility and was prepared to tell all. It was a part of her she had to keep in check.

"You're a great cook," he said, interrupting her thoughts, and gesturing toward what was left in the serving dishes. "This was wonderful."

"I'm great at following recipes. I'm not so sure that's the same thing as being a great cook." She placed her knife and fork on her empty plate. "I got this one from Corinne. It's not bad. Goat cheese and all."

"I was teasing about the cheese, by the way," he said, finishing off his wine.

What he was doing was trying to make her feel better. "Sure you were."

He frowned, shook his head, swallowed. "I swear. It's one of my faves."

She laughed, moving her napkin to the table from her lap. "You are so full of crap."

"What I'm full of is dinner. I have no idea where I'm going to put dessert."

"We can save it," she suggested, loving the disheveled style of his light-brown hair, the sexy stubble covering his jaw. Loving even more how he looked in her kitchen, how right it felt having him here.

"Are you kidding me? Save Italian cream cake?"

Laughing, she got to her feet, stacked their plates, and gathered up their utensils, feeling incredibly nurturing and enjoying it more than she should. "Why don't I make coffee? We can have dessert in the living room."

"In front of the fire?" Caleb stood and pushed his chair beneath the table. "Like a date?"

"Since that's what this is, yes," she said, then carried the dishes to the sink. When she turned to head back for the rest, he was there behind her, trapping her against the edge of the counter.

"What are you doing?" she asked, feeling the flutter of her pulse in her throat.

"Dating."

She looked down to where he'd pressed his lower body against hers, the flutter moving lower and turning insistent, urgent. "It's been a while, but I'm pretty sure this isn't the dating I remember."

"It's grown-up dating," he said, grinding against her, reaching for the buttons of her blouse and pressing his lips to the base of her neck.

"I see," was all she could get out. She was too focused on the way her skin zinged beneath his hands and mouth to say more, and instead of reaching for him the way she wanted, she held on to the counter's edge by her hips.

She longed to touch him, she did, but she ached with the way he touched her. He stroked and pleasured and made love to her, revered her, with every movement of his fingers, every ministration of his lips and his tongue. His touch made her want to cry. She hadn't felt this treasured, this desired in so long.

She closed her eyes, dropped her head back on her shoulders, shivered when he reached under her short skirt and slipped his fingers beneath the leg opening of her panties. He rubbed the bare lips of her pussy, bumped his knuckles back and forth over her clit.

She spread her legs wider, wanting his penetration, needing to feel him moving inside of her, but he continued to tease her, his hand in her panties, his mouth moving down to kiss the swell of her breasts above the lace edge of her bra.

She couldn't take this. She needed more skin-to-skin

contact, more friction, more heat, and less—she couldn't believe she was thinking it—foreplay. She parked her hands on his shoulders and shoved. "I'm tired of dating. If you don't mind, I'd rather just go to bed."

His eyes sparked when he laughed, a deep rumbling growl of a sound that told her he was all for playing along. "What about coffee and dessert?"

She kicked off her wedge heels, reached back and unzipped her skirt. The garment fell to her feet and she kicked that away, too. She left her blouse hanging open, and stood there in her panties and bra. "You can have cake and coffee, or you can have me."

She didn't give him a chance to do anything but narrow his eyes and devour her with a look. She lifted her chin and walked by him, leaving her shoes and skirt in the kitchen, dropping her blouse in the hallway, unhooking her bra and draping it over the knob of her bedroom door.

She had just shimmied out of her panties and crawled up the bed on her hands and knees when Caleb caught up with her and covered her body with his. He was as naked as she was, and didn't ask or pretend not to know what she wanted. He mounted her from behind, his sheathed erection sliding into her, and she was wet and swollen and ready.

She groaned, pressed her forehead to the mattress, clutched the comforter as if she needed the anchor to keep her from flying off the bed. Caleb held her hips, pushing in and pulling out with maddeningly slow thrusts, causing her senses to spiral wildly, her arousal to consume her.

He leaned over her, slipped one hand from her hip to her belly, then lower still to her clit. He pressed against the knot of nerves coiled there, caught it between his forefinger and thumb, pinched, rolled and tugged until she whimpered and writhed. She couldn't believe he was giving her this, that he was so focused on pleasing her.

"Come, Miranda."

She shook her head on the mattress. She wasn't ready. "Not yet. This feels too good."

"There's always more of this to be had. Anytime you want it. Come for me, Miranda. I want to feel you let go."

Oh, but how she wanted to do just that. She slid forward until she was flat on the mattress. Caleb slid with her, his cock still inside her, his hand caught between her body and the bed. She lifted her hips to give him room to move, but instead of pulling free, he continued to touch her, his fingers playing while his cock stroked.

She wanted to turn over, but later. When they were done here. When he didn't have the upper hand. When she wasn't feeling this mad rush of emotions. She'd turn over then, wrap her legs around his hips, and search his gaze for what he was feeling...

He had to be experiencing at least some of the same sense of rightness overwhelming her, didn't he? Or was she truly feeling all of this alone? This connection, this perfection. This powerful thing they had found that was growing too large for her heart to contain.

She shifted her position, moved one hand down between her legs to join his, spreading her fingers in a V around his cock where it entered her. He groaned, thrust, muttered sexy threats and sexier promises under his breath.

"Come for me, Caleb. I want to feel you let go."

This time he didn't mutter, but spewed a string of raw words and curses into the air as he pumped his hips, filling her, stretching her, pleasuring her until she couldn't hold back. She cried out, shuddering, her muscles contracting to milk him as he came, too.

It was bright and brilliant, explosive and fast. She was still shaking when he pulled out and flipped her over, shoving inside her again while they lay face-to-face. Tears rolled from the corners of her eyes. She hadn't meant to release them. She'd tried so hard to keep the things she was feeling tucked away.

But he cupped her face in his hands and smiled at her, brought his mouth down to kiss her, and she was lost. She wrapped her arms around his neck and held him close, fighting one sob, then another, until everything she was feeling spilled out in the most ridiculously loud hiccup.

She couldn't decide whether to laugh or to weep with joy that what had started to feel like a monster intent on ruining the rest of the night, dissipated with that ungodly sound.

"Sorry about that," she said, then hiccuped again and laughed when it wouldn't stop. "I think that was all my veggies being tossed around."

"Bell peppers, definitely," he said, rolling away now that he'd softened.

She brought up her hand to cover her mouth. "Oh, gross."

"Hey." He propped up on one elbow, comfortable in being naked beside her. "Not gross. Just the same thing I'm tasting."

"Note to self. No sex after salad."

"How 'bout sex before dessert?"

"Coming right up," she said, pushing into a sitting position, not quite as comfortable as he was, fearing her emotions were as exposed as her skin.

Caleb grabbed her arm before she could scoot off the bed. "Miranda. It's okay."

"No, it's not." She didn't want to talk about this now. Not the truth, anyway. "I'm a terrible hostess with terrible manners."

"Maybe so," he said, dragging her back for a long earthy kiss. "But you're a hell of a date."

# 14

CALEB LAY SPRAWLED on his side on the Persian rug that covered the living room's hardwood floor. He'd set Miranda's coffee mug on the low table, and was sipping at his own while waiting for her to follow with the cake.

He'd pulled on his socks for warmth, and his jeans, boxers and dress shirt for propriety, but had left the latter unbuttoned just in case she got an itch to scratch him.

Instead of dressing in the clothes she'd been wearing, Miranda had put on skinny black pants, socks and a sweater, and had scooted around him in the kitchen while making coffee as though she was skating on a floor of ice.

He'd been afraid she was going to fall down and break an arm or a leg, but not half as afraid as he'd been of her heart breaking while they'd made love. He'd been well aware of the hitch in her breathing, the way she'd been reluctant to put distance between them but had. Just because he wasn't keen on emotions didn't mean he was clueless about feelings.

Especially women's feelings.

Especially women's feelings about sex.

Miranda hadn't been with a man in a while. He didn't know anything about her history, whether she was divorced or had never married, whether she'd gone through a bad breakup or parted ways amicably with the men she'd dated at the ends of their relationships, whether short-term or long.

He didn't know any of that, but he didn't have to. All that mattered was how right it felt for her to be with him. And the fact that it did made his leaving on Monday a good thing for them both. She didn't need a man in her life with the means to expose whatever it was she didn't want known. And he could do that in a very big way.

He wasn't planning to, but then he hadn't been planning to with Delano Wise either—though it was Del's fiancée Caleb had really screwed over, betraying a confidence to tell the world about the Christian music phenomenon's cocaine addiction and stint in rehab. Thanks to his Max Savage exclusive, she'd lost her recording contract and a deal for her own clothing label with a national department store chain.

And Caleb? He'd lost the best friend he'd ever had, a massive chunk of his self-respect and the blinders he'd been wearing, ones that had kept him from seeing that over the years he had, indeed, done harm. That there was a line, and he'd crossed it. That there were boundaries, and he'd gone beyond them, changing himself in the process.

"Are you sure you're in the mood for cake?"

He hadn't heard Miranda come into the room, and he looked up to see her standing with two plates in her hands. He swung up into a sitting position and reached for one. "I'm always in the mood for cake."

"You looked lost in something pretty intense," she said, neatly folding her legs and dropping down beside him.

He shook his head, dug off a bite of the top layer with his fork. "Thinking about a book I'm working on."

"You're writing a book?"

This was probably as good a time as any to reveal one or

two of his true colors. Since she'd had a bad experience with the press, he knew what he did would make a difference to anything that might happen between them. "When I said I worked in the arts, that was a bit of a stretch. I work in entertainment news."

She froze. Her eyes went wide, and he caught a glimpse of the fear he'd wondered about before. "You're a reporter?"

He nodded.

"You said you worked in the arts."

"I know. The arts just sounded less…"

"Tawdry? Shallow? Mindless? Cheap?"

He feigned collapse. "Way to cut out a man's heart."

"You expected kudos and admiration?" she asked, staring at her cake before brutally stabbing at the slice with her fork.

Why did he feel as if she would rather be stabbing him? "I write a mean story."

"*Mean* being the operative word," she said, finally cutting off a bite.

He took a swallow of his coffee, needing a bit of distance before responding. "I write an entertaining story, then."

"And you use the most entertaining details whether they're true or not."

Firing back wasn't going to earn him any points, but damn if having her pin him like a butterfly didn't sting. "You really know how to stick it to a guy, don't you?"

"I'm sticking it to what you do, not who you are," she told him before popping the cake into her mouth.

He couldn't separate himself from his work that easily. He'd be surprised to find out that she could. "So if I were to call Candy a karaoke hack, Miranda wouldn't wince just a little bit?"

"Maybe a little," she admitted, then sobered, her brow

furrowed as she went back to thinking, drinking her coffee, thinking, eating her cake, before finally asking him, "Why entertainment news, then? Why not Capitol Hill or the Middle East—"

"Instead of Hollywood and New York? Since what I report on isn't really important? Or even news? No matter how many people gobble it up?" Yeah, he'd heard it all before.

She nodded, avoided making eye contact. "What you do hurts people, Caleb."

He knew he was feeling too defensive over something he was walking away from, but he still viewed the work he'd done as having value—even if he'd made a mistake and lost his taste for it, lost his ability to draw the lines.

"All reporting has the potential to hurt people, Miranda. I reveal a scandal on Capitol Hill, someone's going to get hurt. I report on American deaths in the Middle East, someone's going to get hurt."

"But it's not the same. Not at all. Don't you see that?" she asked, punctuating her insistence with a sharp stab of her fork to her plate.

"It's not the same because you were hurt in your former life by some journalist, is that what you mean?" he asked, sensing he was close to tripping over the root of her anathema for his brand of news.

"My divorce, yes. I was humiliated, made out to be a pitiable figure who either couldn't keep her husband satisfied, or whose charitable works were to throw investigators off the scent of his fraud. Take your pick, and add an icy-cold bitch to the list while you're at it."

So there *was* another name to go with Miranda Kelly. A name, a divorce, an ex-husband accused of fraud. "It's human nature. People want to see the mighty fall. It makes it easier for them to feel better about their own situations. And you're not icy or cold."

"A thought or two for the mighty who share that human nature would be nice." She took a deep breath. "Sorry. That sounded arrogant and pathetic all at the same time."

"Something only one of the mighty could accomplish," he said teasingly, watching the play of the firelight as it caught the lighter strands of red in her hair.

"Trust me," she said with a snort. "I was never mighty. I happened to marry well. That's all."

"Doesn't sound like that's the case. Not if he cheated."

"The cheating came later. He developed an inflated sense of self-importance and the entitlement that went along with it. What he wanted, he made sure he had."

"But he quit wanting you."

"No. I quit wanting him. I'd become the dutiful wife, busy with my own causes, with running our household…I never knew about the other women until his philandering came out in the trial."

"The trial?"

She waved him off with her fork. "I've said too much. How's the cake?"

"The cake is great." And to his way of thinking, she hadn't said enough.

"Finish telling me about your book," she said, obviously hoping to derail his prying.

But her reaction to what he did had him feeling rather protective of his future plans. "I'm not sure that I want to."

"I promise, no sticking it to you, or to what you do. I want to hear about what you're writing. Really."

He doubted that, but talking about his study on the tabloids' impact on society should keep him off her hit list.

He just wasn't sure how much of his plans for the future he wanted to share with anyone.

He surprised himself by starting out with a full confession. "Considering everything I just said, this is going to sound really strange, but I'm actually working at getting out of the industry."

She gave him an appropriately stunned look. "Is this book how you'll do that?"

He nodded. "I'm putting together a proposal for my agent to shop. He's already giddy at the prospect of an auction."

For several tense seconds, she stared at him thoughtfully, then said, "I think there's something you're not telling me about who you are."

Uh-oh. "Why would you think that?"

"You seem awfully confident this book is going to be big."

With the information he had at his disposal? He knew it would be big. "We'll have to get together one day and trade secrets."

She blew out a huff of breath. "Probably not a good idea. I can't imagine anyone who'd want to clean up after that explosion."

He laughed. "I'll just send you an autographed copy of the book before it hits the shelves. How's that?"

"Can I ask you something?"

"Sure."

"It's none of my business, and I have absolutely no right to expect you to answer—"

"Ask me, Miranda. If I don't want to answer, I won't."

"If you had the choice, would you rather be writing for CNN or the *New York Times?*" She paused to let him assimilate what she'd asked him before adding, "Instead of covering celebrity weddings, which I'm assuming is what you're here to do rather than just attending the event?"

And here she'd said she wasn't going to stick it to him again. "I am, yes, and I'll answer the first part if you'll answer a question for me."

She stiffened, but she met his gaze directly, her green eyes sparkling from the firelight and the sizzling heat of her emotion. "What do you want to know?"

"Why did you move back here?"

"What do you mean?" she asked, frowning. "This is where I grew up."

"But you left, you got married and divorced, and you came back. Why?" He reached for his coffee, brought it to his mouth.

She shrugged as if she thought the answer should be obvious. "I like it here. It's quiet, peaceful, wonderfully stress-free."

He pushed harder. "And there's no press hounding you?"

"That's part of it, yes," she said, nodding. "But I don't expect you to understand what it's like to be hounded. You're on the wrong side of the microphone."

He thought back to what she'd asked him, back to what she'd told him about her divorce before that. "Would it make a difference if my microphone were recording for CNN or the *New York Times?* Is it just the entertainment part of what I do you don't like?"

"It's hard for me to take in, that that's who you are or what you do. You represent everything I hate about the media. And yet…"

"And yet you can't find it in you to tell me to go."

"I can't. I enjoy your company. I like being with you. I thought… Never mind." She shook her head, tears glistening in her eyes. "It doesn't matter."

It did matter, but he wasn't going to argue or say anything else to upset her. If she didn't want to see him again, he wasn't going to push. But he couldn't help but wonder how she'd react if she knew the whole truth instead of the sanitized version he'd given her.

"If you don't mind, I'm going to turn in. I suddenly have a terrible headache," she said, then set aside her plate and got to her feet, hugging herself tightly. "The guest room is all yours, or there are pillows and blankets in the closet if you'd like to sleep in here with the fire."

"Sure," Caleb said, wondering if screwing up the important things in his life was karma biting back because of the way he'd screwed up the lives of so many others. "I'll see you in the morning. Good night."

# 15

WHEN CALEB FINALLY dragged his butt off the couch the next morning and made his way to the bathroom, he found a note from Miranda propped up on the back of the commode. She'd prepped the coffeepot, all he had to do was turn it on.

There were eggs and hot cereal if he wanted to cook break fast, cold cereal if he wanted to keep it simple. She was at the flower shop, but would see him tonight at Club Crimson if he felt like making up for last night. That made him smile. Then it made him cringe and feel like the jerk he was.

Since she hadn't offered him use of the shower, he skipped doing more than washing his face and using his finger for a toothbrush. He should've come prepared to spend the night, but he'd only come prepared for sex and dinner.

He did, however, take her up on the coffee, drinking almost the full pot while standing in her open kitchen door and freezing his balls off. It was one of those pleasure-pain things that was hard to explain. The hot coffee made the icy cold bearable— if anything about where he found himself this morning was.

First things first. He'd decided before drifting off last night to pay a visit to Under the Mistletoe and send Miranda a bouquet to thank her for the wonderful meal and an evening he wouldn't soon forget. The irony of her having to send flowers to herself was hardly lost on him.

Either she'd appreciate the gesture as the mea culpa it was, or he'd be further inflating his jerkitude factor in her eyes. And in that case, he doubted there would be any making up going on.

First he had to figure out where the flower shop was and how to get there from here. He found the phone in her kitchen, with a business directory in a drawer beneath, and Under the Mistletoe listed as the only local florist.

The address was on First Street, which according to the tiny map at the bottom of the ad, really was the next street over from Second Avenue. Unfortunately, the number of the address was 102 which, if Mistletoe's numbering system ran like those in most cities, put him walking ten blocks in the cold.

He had his boots and his coat, but he didn't have a hat or pants warmer than his jeans. He'd have to move fast, rely on his circulation to keep him warm and hope, in the process, he didn't lose his ears and nose to frostbite.

Once he got started, he realized it really wasn't that cold. Or maybe he was too busy trying to come up with a way to repair the damage he'd done last night to notice. Even though she'd smacked on him, his doing the same to her had been unconscionable.

She wasn't the cynic he was. She believed in love and romance and no doubt in happily ever after, too—even after going through what had sounded like the sort of divorce that cured most people from believing in fairy tales.

It didn't surprise him, not really, that she still did. She was kind, smart, sweet, an optimist—all the things he wasn't.

Well, he *was* smart. And intuitive; he wouldn't be the success he was if he didn't have a brain—though that might be hard to prove based on this cold-weather trek he was making.

Boy Scout material he was not, he mused, looking down at the snow crusting the toes of his boots.

He still couldn't believe she'd left him to find his own way out of the inn's supply room. It was more understandable that she'd made him sleep on the sofa, though that had gotten to him, too. After all, he thought, as a gust of wind smacked him, not two hours before giving him the boot from her bed, she'd given him her body.

She could sing, she could cook, she could run a business. She was every man's dream in bed and was gorgeous to boot. If he wasn't careful, he mused, cupping his hands and blowing into them to keep his fingers from falling off, he was the one who was going to start believing in relationships and other L-words than lust.

Five minutes later he reached the one-hundred block of First Street and found Under the Mistletoe tucked between Orsy's Donuts and Hardware by Frank. He reached up to smooth down his hair, then reached back and messed what he'd straightened.

When he stepped through the front door he heard two female voices—one Miranda's, the other most likely Brenna Sparks's mother. The one he didn't recognize was saying something about Zoe staying after school to meet with the Christmas dance committee and Patrice giving her a ride home.

Caleb tucked those tidbits into his mental file and headed for the counter, the chime over the door silencing in mid-ring as the door shut behind him. It was the Sparks woman who came out of the back to help him with a cheery "Good morning."

"Good morning." She looked a lot like Brenna around the eyes, but her mouth was pinched and aged, even while her smile was welcoming. "I need to order some flowers. Do you deliver to the Inn at Snow Falls?"

"We do, yes. Do you know what you want? Can I help you decide on something?"

Though he was sure she could hear him, Miranda kept herself hidden. All the better to tease her with his dastardly plan. "Do you know Candy Cane? The singer at Club Crimson?"

Corinne stared down at her order pad, tapping with a pen as if trying not to give too much away. "I do, yes. Is that who you're sending this to?"

He nodded. "I'm not so good with knowing what a woman might want. Uh, when it comes to flowers, I mean. Roses seem too over the top, and plants seem too…funereal. What would you recommend? What do you think she would she like?"

"Well, that depends on what you want to say," she said, doodling a cane at the end of Candy's name. "'Enjoyed the show' or 'Thanks for the memories' or 'Same time next year'?"

Caleb struggled to keep from revealing any more than Miranda might have already shared of their affair. "Maybe all of the above with some added—'Sorry for being a jerk'?"

"'Enjoyed the show,'" Corinne quoted back as she scribbled on the pad, adding, "'Thanks for the memories.' 'Same time next year.' 'Sorry for being a jerk.'" Then she met his gaze, her eyes twinkling. "Anything else?"

"Yeah. 'You made me love goat cheese.'"

"Got it," she said, almost laughing now, reaching up and nudging one knuckle against her nose. "Let me think what would best convey all those sentiments."

They talked for several minutes, Corinne suggesting a variety of flowers to go into an exotic arrangement, and Caleb whipping out his credit card without a care for the cost. It would be worth whatever they billed him to imagine Miranda assembling her own flowers or watching her employee arrange the bouquet, knowing it was for her.

As he looked up from signing the receipt, a movement caught his eye, and he cut his gaze to where Miranda stood in the entrance to the shop's back room.

She had her arms crossed over her chest, a shoulder propped against the wall, and was wearing blue jeans, a sunflower-yellow turtleneck and an apron embroidered with her shop's logo. She shook her head, her look as she met his eyes telling him she could not believe what he'd done.

He winked back, stuffed the receipt into the bill compartment of his wallet, and turned to Corinne. "The donut shop next door. Do you know how late they stay open? Or is there another place close by where I can get a cup of coffee while I wait for the inn's shuttle?"

"Orsy is open till noon at least. Sometimes later, depending on the crowd." She motioned him closer, leaning across the counter. "Don't tell him I told you, but he's good about throwing together sausage biscuits for people who need more in their stomachs than pastries."

"Thanks," Caleb said, waving at Corinne as he headed for the door, but looking at Miranda as he said, "And your secret's safe with me."

Orsy's Donuts gave Caleb a sugar high the minute he walked through the door. The small eatery was obviously a gathering place for locals taking midmorning breaks. The customers were mostly male, mostly dressed in aged denim and thick down, and mostly over sixty.

At the long Formica counter, Caleb climbed onto a stool that swiveled when he sat. He clenched his fingers, blew into his cupped hands. That got him the attention of the wiry man behind the bar who walked toward him with a large white mug and a coffeepot.

"I've learned to ask before I pour," said the man with a badge that read Orsy pinned to his apron. "Some people who come down from the inn want juice or tea instead."

"Coffee. Cream. Sugar. I love all the things that I shouldn't," Caleb said, nodding his head toward the mug and inhaling the fragrant steam as the other man poured.

"What about something to eat?" Orsy asked, leaving room in the cup for Caleb's extras. "Donuts, Danishes, turnovers. Pick your poison."

"Anything with cream cheese would be great." Caleb reached for the sugar shaker, cutting his gaze toward the other man while adding two teaspoons worth of sweetener to his drink. "Maybe a sausage biscuit or two?"

Orsy snorted and set a handful of individual creamers next to Caleb's mug. "You've been talking to Corinne, haven't you? I make biscuits one time for her as a favor, and she tells everyone she sees they're an off-menu item."

Caleb dumped three of the creamers into his coffee and stirred. "Hey, a cream cheese Danish is fine. I was thinking to knock out both breakfast and lunch with one stop, but I'll find a burger later."

"Oh, I'll get you the biscuits," the bakery owner said, dismissing Caleb's decision with the wave of his empty hand. He returned the coffeepot to the warmer, coming back with a Danish the size of the saucer he served it on. "Only good place for burgers is Fish and Cow Chips, and Finch doesn't open till four. Unless you want the fast-food type down at the McDonald's. I'll get you those biscuits. You just hold on."

Caleb picked up the Danish and bit in, then picked up his

coffee and drank, reaching, as he did, for a paper that turned out to be Mistletoe's weekly local news.

He flipped through the ten or so pages to get a feel for the content, then started at the beginning and read through. There were a couple of national stories, some county political flare-up, a report on Denver's crime lab and a lot of snowfall predictions for local ski runs.

He found an ad for Miranda's shop in the classifieds, and wondered how much of her business stemmed locally as opposed to from the Inn at Snow Falls. He had to think the lovers' resort would provide a good chunk of her revenue, because in a town as small as Mistletoe he was surprised to see a florist at all.

Then again, he supposed people honored birthdays, anniversaries, births, deaths and holidays everywhere on the map. Just because he wasn't much of a flower giver didn't mean there weren't others who spent a fortune on the things.

Listening to the chatter around him, he found himself smiling as he thought about the card accompanying Miranda's bouquet. He doubted many florists were asked to include notes about goat cheese, though there were probably a lot who were asked to include apologies.

Next time he saw her, he'd offer another via voice. Her smile as she'd watched him pay for the order was enough to let him know his point had been made. Still, he would prefer delivering his mea culpa face-to-face.

This whole incident was a big fat perfect reminder of why emotions got in the way of good times, he mused, thanking Orsy with an acknowledging nod when he delivered his food and topped off his coffee.

Here they were, he and Miranda, having known each other three days, having shared dinner, drinks and sex—and she was already banning him to the sofa, while he was already sending her flowers to make up for doing her wrong.

It bugged him even to go into rights and wrongs, a situation he mulled over as he bit into the sausage biscuit and swore he'd died and gone to breakfast heaven. Caleb was being himself. That was all.

Miranda liked him well enough in bed, seemed to enjoy herself when the conversation stayed in the shallow end of the flirtation pool, but when things moved away from the easy and the safe into the deep and the dangerous…

He'd meant what he'd told her. Any news story published had the possibility to hurt someone somewhere. He understood she was operating from a place of having suffered that hurt, but her blaming those who did the reporting without addressing what the public considered newsworthy didn't sit well with him.

And that fundamental difference in outlook—even though he wasn't particularly proud of how he'd gone about telling every story he'd put on the page—was going to be what kept them apart in the end.

# 16

"OKAY, SPILL," Corinne said, spinning toward Miranda the second the door closed behind Caleb and the chime stopped. "What's the deal with the flowers? And does he know who you are?"

Miranda leaned a forearm on the wall, leaned her forehead on her forearm. "He knows, yes."

"You told him?"

"No," she said with a snort, looking up and gesturing with one hand, not even sure who she was most aggravated with: Caleb, herself or Barry. "It was Barry, fancying himself as tour guide to Mistletoe, Colorado's stars or something."

Corinne picked up the order pad and read from the notes she'd written while Caleb had talked. "Goat cheese and sorry for being a jerk?"

"It's a long story." Miranda turned back to the work room. She wasn't sure she wanted to go into it with Corinne, and have her friend lecture her on getting so deeply involved with Caleb in such a short amount of time when she'd sworn off getting involved with strangers at all.

And they *were* deeply involved. As much as she hadn't wanted it to happen. As much as she knew *he* hadn't wanted it to happen.

"Well, since I've still got the wedding flowers to finish on top of everything else, you talk and I'll listen." Corinne set Caleb's order aside and got back to an arrangement of two-dozen red roses also slated for delivery to the inn. "I'm going to take a wild guess and say the stuffed chicken turned out okay?"

"It was more than okay," Miranda assured her, boosting up to sit on her bar stool. "And the cake I bought at Ida's? Amazing."

"Italian cream?"

Miranda nodded, her accompanying moan near orgasmic.

Corinne sighed her own appreciation. "Mm-mm-mm. I swear, I owe at least thirty of my extra pounds to Orsy and Ida. And yet I keep going back for more."

"You're not the only one." Miranda booted up her laptop and waited while the accounting program launched. "I want to know how the two of them stay so thin. Their kids, too."

"It's all in the G-E-N-E-S. As opposed to being in the J-E-A-N-S, which seems to be more of a problem for you," Corinne said, and Miranda gave her a look.

"That was a terrible segue."

"Yeah, but it got us back on track."

Miranda pointed to the computer screen. "I'm doing payroll. You might want to rethink what track you're on."

"Just for that," Corinne said, one eyebrow arching, "Candy Cane is going to get the most hideous arrangement Under the Mistletoe has ever designed. There won't be a single flower in it she likes. In fact, it's going to be filled with the ones she most hates."

At that, Miranda had to laugh. "I guess it's a good thing she's not allergic to much of anything or one sniff and she'd end up in anaphylactic shock."

"I was just wondering about that," Corinne said, shelving the roses in the cooler. "But since I can't afford to get fired if I want to fund whatever part of Zoe's education her scholarships won't cover, I guess I'll put together something nice."

"You haven't mentioned if she's decided where she's going to go." Miranda knew Zoe had been accepted by all three schools to which she'd applied. All amazing universities. All on the East Coast. All very far away from Corinne. "I know it's going to be hard on both of you, wherever she goes."

Corinne brushed off Miranda's attempt at comfort, sorting through the vases kept on hand for the more exotic arrangements. "Zoe will be fine. Zoe will be super, in fact. She's looking forward to leaving Mistletoe and getting a taste of the real world, as she calls it."

"And you?" Miranda asked, not surprised by the deflection.

"Mc?" Corinne asked, once again considering herself as an afterthought. "I'll survive."

Miranda wasn't having it. "You'll do more than survive. You'll do all the things you've been putting off because of the demands on a single parent rearing an exceptional child."

Corinne responded to that with a snort. "You mean like cleaning out the garage and grouting the bathroom tile? Yep. Can't wait."

"You said you wanted to spend a week with your sister in Boston. And you and May Potter were talking about an Alaskan cruise." Corinne had always put her girls first, but to have nothing of her own to look forward to was new, and a change that concerned Miranda. "You have paid vacation time, you know. I mean, if you're worried about losing the hours."

"I'm not worried about the hours."

"Then what?" Miranda asked, turning to sit sideways on the chair and giving her friend her full attention.

Facing the shelf of vases but staring off into space, Corinne released a sigh that shook her whole body. "I'm worried that I've screwed up so badly with Brenna that Zoe won't forgive me for it, and neither one of my daughters will ever come home again."

"What are you talking about?" Miranda asked, sliding from the chair and crossing to where her friend stood. "Of course Zoe will come home."

Her eyes damp, Corinne cut a questioning gaze in Miranda's direction. "And Brenna? I mean, I haven't exactly showed her open arms, but what if she eventually stops trying?"

"Then you'll go to her and you'll make the effort. She's here now."

"At the inn, yeah," Corinne said, shaking her head and reaching for a squat vase colored an iridescent coral. "But I only know that because people have seen her and told me. It's not like she called and let me know."

Brenna could've chosen anywhere in the world for her wedding to the congressman. Miranda couldn't believe her coming to Mistletoe was about anything but wanting her family with her on such an important day.

But she was still practically a girl, one with a formidable force of a mother. "Maybe she's afraid to come any closer."

Corinne frowned, hugging the vase to her chest. "Why would she be afraid?"

"I don't know. Maybe because you've given away her gifts and refused to take her money." Miranda wrapped an arm around her friend's shoulders. "Maybe she believes all the gossip about you hating her lifestyle."

"I do hate her lifestyle." Corinne pulled away, moved to set the vase on the table. "That doesn't mean I hate her. I could never hate her."

Love the person, loathe their deeds. Learn to compromise. Advice Miranda could afford to take to heart. "Maybe she needs to hear that?"

"I've told her that very thing God knows how many times," Corinne said, her tone cracking under the weight of her internal struggle.

"You could always say it again," Miranda suggested, returning to her computer, smiling as she added, "Maybe this time with flowers?"

"You'll do anything for a sale, won't you?" Corinne asked, but she did revisit the shelf and choose a second smaller vase to go with the one she'd already selected for Caleb's order.

*There are days,* Miranda thought, *when nothing speaks as eloquently—and elegantly—as flowers.* "With the way things have been going today? It sure looks that way."

SINCE HE WASN'T UP for the two-mile walk to Mistletoe County High School, Caleb phoned Barry, the shuttle driver, before leaving Orsy's, and asked if he had time in his schedule for the detour before heading back to the inn.

Barry had nothing lined up, and was glad to play taxi for the tip Caleb offered—as long as Caleb understood he'd have to turn back if dispatch got a call.

He also wanted to know, inquiring once Caleb had climbed into the minivan's backseat, what business Caleb might have at the high school. Not that Barry wanted to cramp Caleb's style—Caleb understood that, right?—he just wanted to be sure there wasn't anything hinky going on with Caleb visiting a high-school campus to see a girl.

Caleb told Barry to rest assured, his visit was strictly work-related, but since he didn't have an appointment, he would appreciate Barry hanging around to make sure he didn't get stuck walking up the mountain to the inn. It was cold, it was getting dark…

Barry was good with all of that, and pulled to a stop at the gymnasium entrance. He'd heard from his wife Marvetta who was friends with May Potter who cochaired the Christmas dance committee with Patrice Price that they held the meetings in the gym so they could work on decorating the place once they were done going over their planning.

Caleb thanked the driver for the scoop, struck with the realization that the information Barry provided for free and in this case to an audience of one, wasn't that much different than what Caleb was paid to provide every day to millions.

It was all a matter of perspective, he mused, stuffing his hands in his coat pockets and heading up the recently shoveled sidewalk to the gymnasium's door. He pulled on the handle, found the door unlocked, and realized again how insulated from the outside world the town of Mistletoe was.

Once inside, he was greeted with a scene from his high-school days, one he knew almost anyone looking back to their teenage years spent in public education would recognize. Crepe-paper streamers and construction-paper cutouts, tempra paint, glitter and glue were spread across the folding tables set up along the far walls.

Students scurried from one table to the next, giggling and chattering as they worked, their athletic shoes squeaking against the glossy wood surface, and the big room amplifying all the noise. It smelled like school, too. Floor wax and sweaty leather and ink on paper and cafeteria grease.

The only thing that had changed since Caleb had been in school was that a man walking into a gym unannounced wasn't left to his own devices but was challenged.

The woman approaching him now was dressed like a lumberjack but built like Marilyn Monroe. Her long brown hair, pulled back in a braid that hung nearly to her hips, swung when she walked. "May I help you?"

Might as well play this one straightforward. "My name is Caleb McGregor. I'm working on a project for Brenna Sparks and staying up at the inn. I was wondering if her sister might have some time to talk to me."

"I know you," she said, considering him with a frown that said she wasn't sure that was a good thing.

He figured she was Alan's wife, but didn't voice his suspicion. "You do?"

"You're the guy Mir—" She caught herself and started over. "You're the guy my friend who works there was talking about."

Might as well let that cat out of the bag. "Would your friend be Miranda Kelly?"

"I wasn't sure if she'd told you her name. I'm Patrice, by the way," she said, offering him her hand. "Patrice Price."

"Nice to meet you, Patrice. And, yeah. She told me the Miranda part. The shuttle driver added the Kelly."

Patrice shoved her hands to her hips. "Damn Barry. Has to have his nose in everyone's business."

"Don't give him too hard a time," he said, shoving his still-cold hands into his jeans pockets for warmth. "He's the one who knew I could find Zoe here."

"I'll never figure out how he does it," she said, shaking her head, her braid popping back and forth. "Knows who's doing what with whom and where all of the time."

An ability Caleb recognized. "It's an ear-to-the-ground thing."

"Ah, yes." She went back to looking at him as if not sure she wanted to like him. "You're a reporter. I forgot that part."

Word got around fast. He'd only confessed all to Miranda last night. "If only everyone could forget that part."

"You mean Miranda? Your kind gave her hell. Take a look in the mirror before you go blaming her for making you jump through hoops."

"No jumping through hoops yet." Just sleeping on the couch, which he supposed was the same thing. "If you're in the middle of things here, I can go. Maybe you could have Zoe call me at the inn?"

"We're done for the most part," Patrice said, glancing back to where several students had ditched the decorations and were passing a cell phone back and forth and giggling at whatever was on the screen. "Zoe!"

A girl with dark hair and huge blue eyes looked up. She got to her feet and came over in answer to Patrice's wave. "Zoe, this is Caleb McGregor. He's a reporter, and was wondering if you'd have some time to talk to him."

"Me?" Zoe looked from Patrice to Caleb, her stance hard to read, her expression emotionally evasive. In other words, a teenager. "What about?"

Being straightforward had worked with Patrice, so he took the same tack with Zoe. "I'm doing a story on your sister."

At that, her eyes brightened. "My sister?"

He nodded. "I talked to her yesterday and wanted to get your take on some of the things she told me."

"You talked to her?" Bright eyes and bright smile. "Here?"

He nodded. "She's staying up at the inn."

"Oh my God! I can't believe she's here," the girl said, shaking her head frantically, her hair flying around her shoulders as she looked at the coats and backpacks piled against the far wall. "I can't talk now. I've got to go."

Patrice reached for Zoe's arm. "You're riding home with me, remember?"

"I'll ride with Deb. She said she's gotta get to work like ten minutes ago." Zoe turned to Caleb to explain. "She works in the gift shop at the inn."

Caleb didn't want to lose this chance to talk to Brenna's sister, and knew he was crossing a line, but… "Actually, if you want to go to the inn, the shuttle driver's waiting for me outside. I'm sure he won't mind driving you home later. He said he doesn't have anything going on today."

"That would be great," she squealed, nearly leaping into the air. "Let me get my stuff. Oh my God. Oh my God. I can't believe Brenna's home."

With Patrice beside him, Caleb watched her go. Or he watched until Patrice stepped in front of him and snarled, "You're some kind of instigator, aren't you?"

*And…here it comes.* "I thought I was doing her a favor."

Her eyes shooting sparks, Patrice dropped her voice. "Did it occur to you that her mother might not want her to talk to her sister? Or run up to the inn by herself?"

Caleb pulled his cell phone from the holster at his waist and flipped it open. "Do you know the number to the flower shop? I'll call and ask."

Patrice hesitated, as if Caleb had called her bluff. He kept the phone in sight, but pressed on. "She's what? A senior? Six months from now she'll be a graduate, two months after that heading for college."

"That's six months from now. Eight months from now," she added, as if he couldn't do the math. "It's not today when she's supposed to be working on plans for the dance."

"I thought you said you were done here."

"Look, Mr. McGregor," Patrice began, rubbing at her temples. "Zoe is very special. To all of us. She's got an amazing future ahead of her."

"And no one here wants her to spiral out of control like Brenna has allegedly done. I got that. But she's obviously made up her mind to go," he said, then played the trump card he'd just realized he was holding. "Would all of you looking out for her rather she make the trip with her friend Deb there rushing to get to work? Or with reliable Barry in his minivan?"

Patrice crossed her arms, and turned to look at the students on the other side of the gym, obviously fighting an internal battle between protecting her cubs from the predators and letting go of one who was ready to step into the wild.

When she finally looked back, it was easy to see that she wasn't happy to have come to her decision. "Don't be logical and make me like you."

"I try to make sure nobody likes me," Caleb said, exhaling his pent-up hope. "It makes it easier to do my job."

"Should I mention that to Miranda?" she asked, one eyebrow cocked.

"You can tell her anything you'd like," he said, though he couldn't deny the pang that hit him with the admission.

Zoe returned then, wearing her coat, her backpack strap hooked over one shoulder. Patrice walked with them to the minivan, shutting the back door behind Zoe and chatting with Barry while Caleb climbed into the front next to the burly driver.

On the drive to the inn, Zoe and Barry did most of the talking, shooting the breeze like best friends. Since questioning the girl was impossible in front of the local rumor mill, all their talking gave Caleb time to think how best to get what he wanted from Zoe before her reunion with Brenna blew his chance.

By the time Barry pulled into the inn's circular drive and

the young valet, Jacob, opened the door, flirting with Zoe as he escorted her inside, Caleb had come up with what he thought was a workable plan.

Keeping his eye on his charge as she and Jacob stood close and talked near the concierge's station, Caleb picked up the house phone at the end of the front desk and asked for Brenna's room.

Five rings later, the singer picked up. "Yeah?"

"It's Caleb McGregor. Could you meet me at One in Vermillion in thirty minutes?"

"I don't know. Do we have anything else to say?"

"You and me? I think we're good. But I thought you might like to talk to Zoe."

Brenna sucked in an audible breath. "She's here? Zoe's here?"

"She just rode up with me from town."

"Does my mother know?"

"Not that I'm aware."

"Okay. I'm coming down."

"Thirty minutes."

"Screw you and your thirty minutes. I'm coming now," she said before slamming the phone into its cradle.

So much for his plans, he mused, spying a very large arrangement of exotic flowers next to a vase of red roses, and another one of daisies and baby's breath on a table behind the clerk.

He thought about Miranda finding the arrangement in her dressing room when she got to work later. Then he stopped thinking about Miranda altogether. He had to think about Zoe and Brenna and his Max Savage swan song so he could get this story done right, and get this monkey off his back for good.

# *17*

TEN MINUTES INTO PACING her dressing room and waiting for the club to clear after her show, Miranda realized she was wasting time. Caleb knew her as herself, so thinking she had to sneak back and rejoin him as her alter ego was silly.

If anyone else was still there, well, none of them were likely to know her, but she'd make sure no vestiges of Candy remained just in case. Besides, the person she most feared making the connection to the ex-Mrs. E. Marshall Gordon was the person she was on her way to see.

She tugged off her wig and washed off her heavy stage makeup in the dressing room's private bath. Only after running a brush through her hair's short layers, applying a fresh coat of mascara and adding gloss to her lips was she faced with a conundrum—what to wear to join Caleb in the bar?

The clothes she wore to commute up and down the mountain—boots, insulated sweatpants and layers of tops beneath her parka—were hardly appropriate for Club Crimson, which left her with Candy's wardrobe to dig through.

She sang four nights a week, and over time had added enough things to her closet that she could go a whole month before she'd cycled through all the outfits she had. That didn't mean they weren't all recognizable as costumes belonging to Candy Cane, being glitzy and one shade or another of red.

But since she didn't have a choice…

She considered the three dresses she owned with a knee-length hem, deciding on one that would be perfect for a night out. It was strapless with a twist bodice and the appropriate boning to keep it in place, and was made of a rich ruby silk.

She found Caleb sitting in the bar's back booth, the same one from that first night and that first kiss. The one she'd avoided approaching earlier at the end of her show, not certain she could resist his temptation.

She still had some self-preservation instincts—though they were quickly becoming things of the past—and she had to admit with each one she shed, she felt as if she were emerging from a confining cocoon. It was a sense of freedom she'd never expected because she'd never thought herself confined.

Caleb looked up when she slid into the booth opposite him, a cherry martini in her hand. His hair was disheveled, the stubble on his jaw a noticeable shadow around a mouth that wasn't smiling.

"What's wrong?" she asked, lifting her drink to her mouth.

"You didn't kiss me," he said, his expression caught between tormented and teasing. "I thought if I sat here again, I'd get the same action as before."

Ah, that. She returned the glass to the table, laced her fingers and rested them in front of it. "I was afraid I wouldn't be able to stop. Your kisses are rather…addictive. And Candy can't play favorites."

"Says who?" he asked, thanking Alan as the other man replaced his empty glass with a full one.

Miranda waited until they were once again alone. She had several things she wanted to say, but had to get the biggest one off her chest first. "I've been thinking a lot about my reaction to what you told me last night, about you working in entertainment news. I owe you an apology."

He gave a sharp huff. "For what? Being honest?"

"For being rude. Your profession is your choice. I may not like it, but it's obviously something you're good at, and my making a stink was uncalled-for. So I'm sorry. Truly."

"No, Miranda. If there's an apology to be made here, I'm the one who needs to make it."

"You already did. And the flowers were lovely." Beyond lovely, though Miranda was certain she thought that partially because he had sent them. "Corinne wouldn't let me see the arrangement. She hid it until she went out on her afternoon delivery run. I had to wait until I got here to get a look at what she'd done."

"And?"

"They were gorgeous. And you shouldn't have spent all that money. But thank you. I can't remember the last time someone sent me flowers."

"You should have flowers every day."

"I do," she said, plucking the cherry from her drink by the stem. "They're just not mine."

Caleb smiled, looked down, turned his glass in a circle on the table. She watched his hand, studied the length of his fingers, remembering having them on her skin, and was extra glad she hadn't kissed him earlier when just that thought caused her stomach to buzz.

He finally spoke. "Had you planned to open the shop before moving here?"

She shook her head, realizing how decidedly unprepared for her new life she'd been upon leaving Baltimore. She'd come here without a single plan, only the need to come home.

Looking back, she couldn't help but be amazed that she hadn't fallen flat on her face.

She wondered if Caleb could sense that amazement when she shook her head. "No, I honestly didn't know what I was going to do. I had my divorce settlement and my savings, and when I discovered the shop was for sale, I jumped. It just seemed so…safe. So normal. So uncomplicated."

"Did you have experience as a florist? Or running a business?"

"Only if working with caterers counts." Volunteer work was called *work* for a reason. "I used to plan fund-raising events for the charities whose boards I served on. It often felt like a full-time job, but I loved it. It was one of the things I missed most after settling here."

He picked up his glass, took a drink. "Yeah, I can't see a lot of charities around here in need of volunteers."

"Exactly. That's why I established one."

He frowned, obviously curious. "Come again?"

"My divorce settlement was rather…substantial," she said, realizing she'd given him another piece of the past he could use to find her out. Realizing on top of that that she was no longer as worried about him doing so as she had been when they'd first met.

Right now, however, she wasn't going to take the time to figure out why. "After realizing the struggle Corinne was going to have putting Zoe through school, I set up a scholarship fund. There are several stipulations, but basically it assists one student each year who plans to study music, art or creative writing."

"Wouldn't that put you in the news? Make you a local celebrity of sorts?"

Ah, but this was the best part. She grinned. "Not me. Candy. It's the Candy Cane Scholarship for the Arts."

"See?" He lifted his glass, used it to gesture toward her. "I knew you loved the arts."

"My arts, not your arts. But you're right. I do." Drink in hand, she sat back, crossing her free arm over her middle. "It's why I took the job singing. I use the money I make at the club for the fund."

"You're quite the woman, Miranda Kelly. Entrepreneur, entertainer, patron of the arts. And that's not even taking in all the rest of the things you're good for."

"What I'm good for?" She kicked out, found his shin beneath the table. "You're walking a fine line toward never experiencing any of that good stuff again."

He sat up straight and saluted. "Consider me back on the straight and narrow."

She did consider him, wondering about other paths he was walking. "Have you used all your reporter's sources and instincts yet to find out who I am?"

And then *he* considered *her,* his gaze intensely curious as it crawled over her. "I thought about doing a Google search, yeah. But the inn's wireless was out when I got back to the room. I started working, forgot about it, and the next thing I knew, it was time for your show. I never checked again."

That wasn't what she'd expected. She'd thought he would be obsessive about digging in the dirt, wallowing until he'd rooted out the tastiest morsels he could find. Either he wasn't that into her…or she had it all wrong, and he wasn't the bottom-feeder she'd pegged him to be.

She wondered which it was. "You get that involved, do you? In your work?"

His expression softened as if he were indulging a child. "Those columns you see in newspapers and magazines? They don't get written without a lot of involvement. And focus. And discipline. Even when the stories are nothing but entertainment news."

"I recognize curiosity is human nature, but whatever happened to minding one's own business?"

"Where do you draw the line between what's public and what's private? Your charity work obviously made you a public figure, as did your divorce—"

"Right there? Those two examples? That's where I draw the line. I want, I *need* my causes to be in the public eye. But my divorce?" She pressed her palm to her forehead then ran it back over her hair in frustration. "I mean, c'mon. Speculation about what I had done during my visits to the spa? For God's sake, one reporter talked to my waxing technician. She didn't say anything, of course. But what right did he have even to ask her such a thing?"

"The rights granted by the first amendment? Freedom of speech? Freedom of the press? You don't have to like what he asked, but he had the right to do so."

She didn't like it. She didn't like it at all. "Then where do ethics come into play? Or is anything fair game in this age of blogs and YouTube? What about an individual's right to keep her personal hygiene routine out of the news?"

"I'll need a history refresher. I can't remember a personal hygiene amendment."

"You're not funny."

"I'm not trying to be. I'm trying to get you to see that you're drawing a line based on your comfort zone."

"And the media docsn't have one, I know."

"The media may not, but there are journalists who do."

"Are you one of those journalists?"

He took longer to answer than she would've expected. She would've thought he knew himself and his work so well that he could draw a line in his own personal sand with his eyes closed and his hands tied behind his back.

"I haven't always been, no," he finally said, his voice low, gruff. "And I haven't always worked in…the arts. I was that college graduate with the journalism degree who was going to save the planet from global warming. Or at least from turning a blind eye to what was happening around the globe. The poverty. The hunger. The religious oppression."

"What made you switch course?"

"I couldn't catch a break. Granted, I was impatient. I wanted my Pulitzer *now.* But every time there was breaking news, I was on the wrong continent, or tied up on assignment in another state. A classic case of always being in the wrong place at the wrong time. What I was bringing to the table in comparison, nobody gave a crap about reading. And then along came Delano Wise."

"The country-music star? That Del Wise? You know him?" When Caleb nodded, Miranda gasped. She remembered the flurry of publicity that had helped launch the singer to stardom. "What does Del Wise have to do with the direction your career took?"

"We grew up together. Played Little League. Punked each other in school. Shared our first cigarette and hated it. Shared our first beer and loved it. Must've been all of twelve."

"You're kidding."

"God's honest truth. When he was on the verge of hitting it really big, I used what resources I had available to keep his name in the news. The more popular he got, the more I did to get him that exposure."

"So it started with Del and now here you are with Teddy and Ravyn. And in helping a friend, you found something that got people's attention, and you offered them that instead of the global warming reports."

"That about sums it up," he said, taking one sip then another before returning his glass to the table.

"Must be a trip to be able to make or break a career with what you keep out of the papers and what you expose."

He shifted, then leaned forward. "You may not like it, but sensationalism sells. Add sex to the mix often enough, you've made yourself a name as the go-to guy for the best gossip to be found."

"How did that make you feel?"

"Honestly? I felt great. I'd made it. On top of the world, and all that."

"And yet…"

"Who said there was a yet?"

"You did. You're a journalist with a comfort zone, remember?"

"It's newly found, trust me. It hasn't always been there."

That sounded like a story she wanted to hear. "It's never too late to make a new start."

A corner of his mouth quirked. "Now you're quoting platitudes?"

"No. I'm speaking from experience," she told him honestly.

He looked down. "I'm sorry you had to go through that."

"Why? I've loved starting over," she told him without a moment's hesitation.

"Not the starting-over part. The public revelation of things that should've been kept private." He said it as if making an apology. As if he'd been responsible for what had happened to her. Or for a similar wrong.

"Well, thank you," she said, a part of her that should've been stronger, melting. "But I'm pretty sure you wouldn't have cut me any slack if you'd been the one there doing the snooping."

"Like I said," he said with a shrug. "In the wrong place at the wrong time every time."

"It's much better this way." And that was another absolute truth. "If you'd revealed my waxing secrets to the world, we wouldn't be dating. And I would really have hated to miss out on dating you."

"I was just sitting here thinking that it was time for more of that." He pushed out of the booth, reached for her hand and helped her to her feet. "Your place or mine?"

# 18

THOUGH THE DRINKS were on the house, Caleb left a sizable cash tip on the table before following Miranda from the club. Alan, who Caleb had learned was Club Crimson's manager, had stuck around long past closing rather than put an end to their conversation.

The tip wasn't about paying him for his time as much as it was a thank-you for respecting their privacy and giving them the space. It was unexpected, especially since Caleb had seen the wife Alan had waiting for him at home.

He and Miranda crossed the stage and headed first for her dressing room. He got that she wanted to grab her clothes and keys and other personal things before going to his room. He got it, but he didn't like it because it meant a delay in getting her into his bed.

He wanted to get her into bed. He was having all these… feelings, and needed the sex to forget them. Miranda had him thinking about the choices he'd made, had him wondering about where he'd gone wrong, why he'd gone wrong, what had triggered the rush of power that had driven him to step over the line. He didn't like feelings. He liked facts. They were clean. Simple. Feelings were messy and got in the way.

Then again, ignoring what he didn't want to feel had probably been the root of his downfall. He hadn't stopped to consider the people involved because he couldn't. He'd had to think objectively about the stories he told. But if he'd remembered he had a heart and not just a head, he and Del might still be friends, or at least still be speaking.

"See? What did I tell you? Corinne did this whole gorgeous arrangement without letting me even peek."

The flowers on her vanity were the ones he'd seen behind the inn's front desk this afternoon. "Nice."

"They are nice," she said, kicking off her heels then twirling around and launching herself at him to give him a hug. "Thank you again. You really didn't have to."

He hugged her back, enjoying the sensation of her arms around him, her hands in the middle of his back, her breasts pressed to his chest, his heart…tingling enough to make him wonder what it would be like to feel more of this, and to feel it all the time. "Can we not talk about the flowers anymore?"

She pulled back to look into his eyes. "What would you like to talk about?"

"Nothing."

"Nothing?"

"I like to think of myself as a man of action."

"Did you come prepared?"

He held up three fingers like the good Boy Scout he was.

"Then don't think," she said, her green eyes begging. "Act."

Caleb didn't have to be told twice.

He kept one arm wrapped around her, threading the fingers of his other hand into her hair's short layers that he loved seeing so much more than her longer and supposedly sexier wigs. To him, nothing beat the real thing.

And that was his last thought before he lowered his head and slanted his mouth over hers. She tasted like Miranda and her cherry martini. She tasted like he could get used to her. She tasted like he wanted her every day, like having her would make him a better man because she made him think—about what he was doing, about what he'd done.

She moved her hands to his chest, slid them up to his shoulders, slipped her tongue into his mouth. She smiled as she did so. He felt her lips on his, saw the sparkle in her eyes just before she closed them, knew that he was in a world of trouble because he lacked what it would take—strength, willpower…the desire?—to walk away.

And so he quit thinking. He just shut down his mind and let his body take over because, right now, being with her was all that mattered, the only thing he wanted, what he cared about most in the world. She meant more to him than she should after such a short time, and that realization left him wondering where things might go with half a chance.

He found the zipper pull beneath her shoulder blades and tugged it to her rump, coming back up to grip the fabric and ease it down her torso. With her dress bunched at her waist, she shimmied her hips and sent the bright-red garment to the floor, then she started in on his buttons.

Once she reached his belt, she tugged his shirttails free from his pants, and finished with the buttons there before moving to his cuffs. She pushed his shirt away much as he'd done with her dress, leaving her wearing nothing but her panties and strapless bra, leaving him in his boots and jeans.

"You're so amazing," she told him, leaning back and looking him over, though staying in the circle of the arms he'd looped around her neck as she did. She ran her palms across his shoulders, down his chest, over his ribs to his abdomen. "Did you know that?"

He resisted sucking in his gut. "You're blinded by all those martinis you drank."

"Am not," she said, shaking her head, her eyes tellingly damp when she met his gaze. "Your body's perfect. I love that your hair is always a mess. And that most of the time you need to shave."

He reached up, rubbed at his chin and jaw. "That's because most of time when you see me, my beard's had several hours to grow."

"I like it. I like this hair, too," she said, nuzzling his chest, finding his nipple, flicking it with her tongue. When he jumped, she moved to the other and did it again. Then she rubbed both of them with her thumbs.

He closed his eyes and groaned, sliding his hands down to release the clasp of her bra. With that hindrance out of the way and her breasts bared, it was his turn to torture her—though first he had to get rid of his boots and jeans.

That done, he backed up until his knees made contact with her vanity bench, then straddled it and sat, pulling Miranda around to straddle him. She spread her legs and did, lacing her hands at his nape while finding her balance.

He looked at her then, her short hair, her freckles, her breasts tipped with nipples the color of pink roses, her sex covered by nothing but a scrap of red mesh that matched her bra. "If anyone's amazing, it's you, Miranda Kelly. You're goddamned beautiful."

She dropped her head, tucked her chin to her chest, began to shiver as he stroked the skin of her neck, her shoulders, his fingers tracing the lines of her collarbone before circling the globes of her breasts.

Her gaze was still lowered when she said, "You make me ache, Caleb. You make me want so many things."

He swallowed hard, wishing he knew how to give her more than this, wishing he knew what it was she longed for as he cupped her neck and pulled her toward him, kissing her until neither one of them could see straight.

It didn't take long for his erection to make itself known between her legs. She squirmed, reached down and stretched the elastic waistband of his boxers far enough for him to spring free. Then she scooted up farther on his lap, capturing his cock between them.

"One of us is wearing too many clothes," she said. "And I think that person is me."

He agreed. He also realized he could easily pull her panties out of the way, and that if she was wearing too much, he wasn't wearing enough. "My pants. My wallet. My kingdom for a condom."

She reached down, tugging his wallet from his jeans' pocket. He dug for one of the condoms he'd stashed inside. She took it from him before he'd even tossed his wallet to the floor, tore the packet open and rolled the sheath from the head to the base of his shaft. Then she planted her hands on his shoulders and pushed him back until he was lying on the bench.

With his hips at one end, his head at the other, he fitted, but just barely. He certainly didn't have room to play acrobat or make like a monkey in the jungle. Miranda didn't seem concerned. She swung one leg over and away so she could get rid of her panties, then swung it back and stood with her sex positioned over his.

Wrapping her hands around the sides of the bench just above his shoulders, she lowered her body, sliding the head of his cock through her slick folds until he was wet with her moisture, then taking the full length of him inside herself, grinding her clit against the base of his shaft as she sat.

He watched as she closed her eyes, parted her lips, caught at her lower one with her teeth. And then she began to move, rotating her hips, groaning as the friction between them heated and increased. He held on to her forearms, bucked his hips, crunched his abs and thrust upward.

She hit a rhythm, up and down, up and down. He countered with his own steady strokes, driving in and out until his heart was racing and sweat broke out in the small of his back, the center of his chest, the palms of his hands. He couldn't remember sex ever being this fierce, this close to the bone.

He watched Miranda's chest rise and fall as she panted, her breasts jiggling inches above him, her nipples just out of reach of his mouth. He wanted to taste her, lick and suck her. He wanted to kiss her tits, kiss her lips, kiss her between her legs. He wanted to know all of her. He wanted years to learn her. He couldn't get enough.

She tucked her chin to her chest, pressed her lips together. He felt the change inside her, the tightness, the contractions, the electrical charge. And then she came, tossing her head back, crying out, shuddering above him. She was the most beautiful creature he'd ever seen, and he couldn't hold back.

He surged into her, gripped her thighs, gritted his jaw and came apart. His muscles burned, his chest ached, his orgasm exploded through him as if ripped from his soul. The intensity seared him, the fire roaring through his veins. It took him forever to return to the moment, and when he did, he knew nothing would ever be the same.

Miranda groaned as she moved off him and crumpled to sit on the floor. "As much as I'm a fan of after-sex cuddling, I think I've just ruined my thighs forever."

Caleb sat up. "Your thighs, my abs. I'm too out of shape for gymnastics."

Miranda laughed, reaching for his shirt and slipping it on as if suddenly worried about modesty. "You are not out of shape. I told you. Your body is amazing."

"My body is old and quickly becoming decrepit," Caleb said, getting to his feet and heading for the bathroom to dispose of the condom, snagging his boxers off the floor on the way. He pulled them on before coming back.

Then he stood above her, staring down. "Do you think we could take this party up to my room? Or do you have to rush home to water the plants or something?"

She cocked her head to the side and considered him while she crossed her legs, tugging the tails of his shirt into place over her sex. "I don't have plants to water, a pet to feed or a stove to clean, no. But we're going to have to stop in the kitchen because it's too late for room service and I'm starving."

Caleb's own thighs were feeling rubbery, so he backed up and sat on the bench, reaching for his socks, then his jeans. He held his pants in his hands as he said, "Let me make something for you while you get your things together. Earnesto saw me the other night. I can tell him you sent me."

"You'd do that?" she asked. Her voice was soft as if she was having trouble placing his offer in the context of their relationship.

He was having the same trouble. Especially since he didn't know what that context was. "Sure, why not? I figure after the show, the booze and the sex, the starvation's half my fault."

He wasn't too crazy about the way she was looking at him, so rather than squirm beneath her scrutiny, he put on his pants, found his wallet on the floor, returned it to his pocket.

She didn't move, or offer up his shirt so he could finish getting dressed. No, she went back to playing with the buttons and the placket, giving him glimpses of her body that caused his cock to rise. "You'd better be careful. I might take that as you caring."

That was the biggest problem of all. He did care, but he wasn't ready to let her know. He was having trouble enough admitting it to himself.

And so what he told her when he helped her to her feet and stripped his shirt from her body was, "I care about getting you fed and into bed. Why don't we leave it at that for now?"

# 19

MIRANDA DIDN'T WANT to move. She was warm, relaxed, sated, incredibly comfortable and loathe to leave Caleb. He was spooned around her, his knees tucked up beneath her bare bottom, his arm draped over her torso beneath her breasts, his head next to hers on the pillow.

His slow measured breaths stirred the hair above her ear. It tickled, but she stayed where she was, wondering if she'd ever woken after a night spent with a man—her ex-husband included—feeling as if her life was perfect.

And not because of the sex. Or at least not solely because of the sex. It was so much more. It was…everything. An everything that frightened her for a very good reason.

If she wanted things to move forward with Caleb, she had to come clean, and she did want them to move forward— because she was coming to care for him deeply.

In a million years, she would never have believed it possible for her to give anyone in the media the time of day, much less her body, and now it seemed, her heart. She knew it was too soon, logic said it was too soon. But when did logic have anything to do with love?

Oh, God. This couldn't be love, even if her heart was about to burst in her chest. Love grew out of affection and friendship and caring respect. It did not grow out of sweaty sex in bedrooms and hotel rooms and rooms with nothing to lie on but a bench or a floor.

Yet even as she mulled over that thought, she knew she and Caleb had shared more. They had talked, their conversations going into how she felt about her past more deeply than she'd gone with Patrice or Corinne. And last night?

The man had actually come back from the kitchen with the best club sandwich she'd ever had in her life. Okay, it was just a sandwich, but having him go to the trouble to put it together for her? Then adding a side of bagel crisps and the chipotle tomato cheese spread she loved?

When had anyone other than one of her best friends been so thoughtful? And when was the last time anyone made her wonder if she really was doing the right thing, avoiding the sordidness of what she'd gone through instead of accepting it as the history it was? With Marshall again in the news, wasn't it the perfect time to stop hiding?

Yes, Caleb held fast to his beliefs, but he let her hold fast to hers, challenging her without demeaning her, questioning her without ridiculing her. He let her be herself. Better yet, he liked her as herself.

Marshall had wanted to mold her, to turn her into his ideal. Caleb might not embrace her same causes or share her same views, even like the same books, food or movies, but he hadn't made a single effort to change her.

He hadn't even pressed to find out why she'd hidden herself. And that was the one thing that was troubling her the most. Why wasn't he pressing? Why wasn't he digging? Not that she wanted him to, but why wasn't he trying to figure her out? It was who he was, what he did. Yet he wasn't doing it with her.

Was he trying to protect her? Respecting the boundaries she'd set? Would he put his own curiosity aside and do that?

She couldn't think about it anymore. Not now. She had to get up. The tickle of his breath above her ear was getting to her, and then there was the screaming of her bladder that no mind-over-matter thinking would silence.

She scooted out from under Caleb's arm, found her panties and his shirt, and carried both to the bathroom where she suddenly realized she was freezing. Instead of washing her face and brushing her teeth as she'd planned, she left the garments on the counter and climbed into the tub.

She knew the shower would finish the job of waking Caleb her sliding from bed had started, but since she thought he might want to tell her goodbye, she didn't feel terribly guilty. Besides, the idea of him joining her in the shower, warming her, washing her—

At the sound of the shower curtain's metal hooks sliding back on the rod, she startled, then turned to stare at a very sleepy Caleb as he stepped into the tub. She stared too long. Shampoo ran from her forehead into her eyes.

"Ouch," she yelped, lifting her face to the spray. Caleb came close while she rinsed, wrapping his arms around her middle and nuzzling her nape. She pulled back, swiping her hands down her face. "If you're not careful, you're going to get a mouthful of lather."

He reached up and adjusted the shower to spray over her head and onto his, sputtering as he cleared the soap from his mouth—and then keeping the water for himself. She had to turn and face him, staying in full body contact to keep warm. It was no hardship at all.

"I didn't mean to wake you up," she said, cuddling close to his chest. "At least not at first."

His hands roamed from her nape to the base of her spine. "What changed your mind?"

She shivered. She didn't want to have to leave him and go to work. "I needed someone to wash my back."

"I see."

"You don't believe me?" she asked, breathing him in, rubbing against the wet hair that had matted in the center of his chest.

"Who washes it when you're at home?"

"No one."

"So it never gets washed?" he asked, using his fingers in ways that definitely qualified as dirty.

Warm water and a warm man with warm hands. She could stay here forever. "I've been thinking of hiring someone. A cabana boy maybe."

"They have those up here in the mountains?"

"A ski bum then."

"If you want, I can help you write an ad for the classifieds."

"And here I never thought having a reporter around would come in handy."

"Reporters are handy for more things than you can imagine," he said, and spent the next thirty minutes showing her.

Once they had both caught their breath, soaped, showered, rinsed and dried off, he asked, "What're you doing today?"

She looked over from running a comb through her hair. "I work Saturdays so Corinne can be home with Zoe, though tonight they're both going to be at her daughter's wedding. I'm going to miss it because of the show, so I'll want a full report."

Caleb frowned. "They made up?"

"Who?"

"Corinne and Brenna."

She nodded, reached for the blow dryer, but ended up setting it aside when she saw the deep V of concentration furrowing his brow. "Last night before closing, Zoe came into the shop. She'd been up to the inn, and she brought Brenna back down the mountain."

"That must've been after I talked to them then."

"You talked to Brenna and Zoe?" The Brenna part didn't surprise her. The Zoe part did, though only because she didn't know Caleb had met the younger of the girls. Then she wondered if they'd talked before or after the delivery of Corinne's flowers. "What about?"

He gave a lazy shrug. "Work. Background stuff for the wedding story. The human-interest side."

She bit down on asking him if he really meant the sensationalist, tabloid side. "Did they tell you they were coming to see Corinne?"

Shaking his head, he said, "Last I heard, they were going to Brenna's room to catch up."

Looking down, Miranda toyed with the controls on the blow dryer. "Corinne sent Brenna flowers yesterday. It's the first gesture she's made this whole time."

"It got Brenna to come to her. It obviously worked."

"Corinne was in tears. Sobbing. All three of them were." Miranda smiled. Her eyes misted as she thought back to the group hug that had taken the small family to their knees in the store's back room. She'd felt like an intruder, and knowing Corinne had her own set of keys, Miranda had locked up and headed home, leaving them to their reunion. "I honestly wondered if it would ever happen."

"Zoe told me what Brenna had done. That was a lot to put on her mother."

"It was," Miranda agreed. "But I guess it's true that time heals all wounds."

"It definitely wounds all heels. I know that much."

"Some heels deserve it," she told him.

"We do indeed," he said and before she could insist that she had not been talking about him, he went on. "If you're working today, what are you doing tomorrow?" He stood with one shoulder on the bathroom doorjamb, his arms over his chest, a towel knotted around his hips like a sarong.

She almost couldn't answer for drinking him in, the stubble he hadn't shaved from his jaw, his biceps that bulged where his arms were crossed. "Since the shop is closed, grocery shopping, cleaning, the usual."

"That can wait."

"Says you." She turned back to the mirror and rubbed the moisturizer she'd taken from her dressing room into her face.

"Yes, and me also says for you to pack a bag and bring it with you tonight."

"Where am I going?" she asked, and met his reflected gaze.

"We're spending the night away. I'll make the arrangements."

Away? He was going to take her away? God, just the idea had her hands shaking. "What about the wedding?"

"I'll be finished there by the time your show's done."

"I need to know what to pack. Casual? Dressy?"

"Casual."

"Outdoor casual or indoor casual?"

"You don't need a snowsuit, but bring a jacket."

"Is this like a real-world date? Not a Caleb McGregor date?"

"It's a real-world Caleb McGregor date. How's that?"

"It's perfect. I love…it," she said, barely catching the slip. "I haven't been out of Mistletoe in forever. I'm excited. And feeling incredibly spoiled."

"Spoiled?"

"First you send me flowers. Then you get me food. And now you take me on a date. A real date. Watch out," she added, reaching for the toothpaste, "or I'll start to expect this treatment."

"Don't," he said, shaking his head.

Uh…gulp. What was that? "Don't start to expect it?"

"Not from me," he said, his gaze fierce as it held and studied hers. "I fly out of here on Monday."

Her throat clogged immediately. She almost couldn't find her voice to speak. "To another assignment?"

He shook his head. "Home. To Baltimore. I figure it's time I check my mail, clean the fridge of whatever leftovers were in there when I flew out and have since built competing bacteria colonies. Air the place some before getting to work on my book."

Oh, God. She took a step back, sat hard on the toilet, appreciative of the lid being down, but surprised since everything around her had just flushed away. "Baltimore? That's where you live?"

He nodded. "I've been there about five years, why?"

"No reason."

Except that seven years ago she'd been the queen of the city's charity balls. And that six years ago her husband had been indicted by its courts. And that five years ago, while he was on trial, she'd started divorce proceedings there.

Could Caleb really not know her from any of that?

She jumped back to her feet, finished brushing her teeth and rinsing, then packed her kit of toiletries. "I've got to get out of here."

"What's wrong? Miranda—"

"Nothing. It's just that if I'm going to have time to pack before going to work, I need to hurry home." She said it while thinking that going away with him after the show tonight was probably the worst thing she could do.

Then again, she'd already stepped off that cliff several times, opening herself up, sharing details of her past that he would have no trouble using to find her out.

That he hadn't tried to nail down her identity by now confounded her, but she knew sooner or later he would—just as she knew the smartest thing to do would be to tell him about the ex-Mrs. E. Marshall Gordon herself.

NOT LONG AFTER Miranda left, Caleb's plans to spend the day preparing for the evening's wedding hit a snag. His concentration started giving him hell the first time through listening to his recording of Brenna Sparks, his efforts to focus derailed by a ridiculous distraction, one that hit him at the most inopportune times.

He could smell Miranda everywhere in the room.

He'd ordered room service after she'd left, hoping the aroma of the coffee, of the bacon and the maple syrup he'd poured on his pancakes would make it impossible for him to smell anything else.

It hadn't worked.

Neither had letting maid service in to clean.

Every time he turned to check the written notes from his conversation with Brenna, or got up to pace and listen to the recording of his conversation with the sisters, he would catch a whiff of something sunny and flowery and warm, and his head would wrap itself around Miranda and the things she was making him feel.

It was so bad, and he was feeling so much, that he still hadn't done anything about searching out her true identity. She'd told him she would tell him when it was time, and for some reason he'd decided that was good enough. He was waiting, letting her call the shots—which he supposed was the right thing to do. It was her life after all.

Thing of it was, he'd never cared about the right thing or the wrong thing, only about getting the scoop. Work had been everything since the moment he'd seen his byline on his very first story. Or it had been until the power Miranda had mentioned had gone to his head and he'd crossed a line into territory where he had no business being.

Speaking of stories… He rubbed the back of his neck as he paced, turning over what Zoe Sparks had told him about the hard feelings keeping her mother and Brenna apart. He wondered if Corinne had shared the whole truth of her thieving daughter with Miranda.

Caleb couldn't imagine that being any fun for the younger daughter, to be torn between sibling and parent. That was one dynamic he had yet to witness, the one his research still lacked: the one between Brenna and Zoe and Corinne.

He stopped pacing, thought a moment. If he set up in the chapel even earlier than he'd planned, he might catch the family still celebrating their reunion.

He set about closing up his laptop, securing his notes and recorder in the same case, then hurried to get dressed and cart his audio and video equipment downstairs.

While he was rolling his cases through the lobby on the way to the inn's chapel, Caleb saw Alan Price walk through the front door. He called out, and met the other man halfway. "I need to get my hands on a car. Anywhere to do that around here?"

"In Mistletoe? No." Alan shook his head. "You'll have to get one of the bigger agencies to deliver."

"I was afraid of that."

Alan shook back the shock of hair that covered his forehead, and hefted higher the pack he carried on his shoulder. "You can't get Barry to take you where you need to go?"

Not if he could help it, Caleb thought to himself. "I'm taking Miranda down to Golden for the night. I'd rather not have Barry along."

Price snickered, obviously at the idea of the local gossip sharing the date. Then he grew sober. "Do you think that's a good idea?"

Yeah…that's the reaction he'd expected. "Taking her out of town?"

"Getting her hopes up."

Was that what he was doing? "I haven't promised her anything but a date. I figured it's been a while since she went out for dinner and a movie. And it's not like I'm going to be here for anything long-term."

"You've told her when you're leaving?"

Caleb nodded. "Told her this morning that I fly out on Monday."

"She was okay with that?" Alan asked, his expression a mix of concern and curiosity.

"Why wouldn't she be?" Caleb realized she hadn't reacted much at all except to drop to the toilet lid and sit. "I know you're just looking out for her, but give her some credit for knowing what she wants to do."

"And who she wants to do it with?"

"Yeah. That, too."

"Here," Alan said after a long moment of eye-to-eye contact. He tossed Caleb his key ring. "An electric-blue Toyota FJ Cruiser. I'll get Patrice to come pick me up when the club closes."

"You sure?" Caleb asked, wrapping his fingers around the bundle of keys, warm in his palm.

"As long as you don't go breaking Miranda's heart," Alan said, bringing his hand down on Caleb's shoulder to enforce his warning with his heavy grip.

Caleb doubted that was a promise he'd be able to keep. So he didn't make it. He just said, "Thanks for the use of the SUV."

# 20

If Miranda had been asked to regale friends with the details of her last date, she wasn't sure she'd have been able to do more than assure whomever was asking that there had been no intimacy involved beyond that of friendship.

Though she'd hardly been in the mood for romance, much less sex, she had agreed to have dinner with one or two single men after filing for divorce from Marshall. But since every move she made was paparazzi fodder, she'd either cooked at her new apartment—where no one could get past the doorman to prove what company she was keeping—or she'd included other friends, and they'd gone out as a group.

And all of that had been before her move to Mistletoe. In the five years she'd been living here, she hadn't had a single date. She hadn't even been interested in going out with any of the few men she had met. Not until she'd lost her mind and kissed Caleb McGregor in front of her Club Crimson audience to a round of deafening applause.

Having him pick her up after work on Saturday had saved them time in getting to where they were going—a boutique hotel in Golden within walking distance of all the shopping, eating and artsy things she could imagine crowding into one day.

She would've given anything to have more.

They'd arrived long after midnight, but Caleb had told the front desk to expect them late. Their room had been ready and waiting. They'd fallen into bed and asleep spooned together and clothed in their underthings, making love once the sun had risen to bathe their room in a toasty yellow glow.

Breakfast had been an extraordinary affair of berries and chocolate, syrup and whipped cream, laughter and kisses topping off Belgian waffles, served with hot coffee and bacon in the restaurant around the corner at ten.

They'd done a lot of window-shopping, as there were only a few stores open on Sunday. She had copied down the contact information for a jewelry store displaying a black Akoya pearl necklace that she coveted, and bought an ivory cashmere cardigan from a clothing boutique she'd had to drag Caleb into.

He'd had to drag her into a stationer's where he'd bought himself a limited edition fountain pen. It had an ivory-colored barrel and sepia-toned scrimshaw artwork that depicted Herman Melville's *Moby Dick,* and he'd given her the matching roller ball to use in her shop.

She'd started to tell him that she couldn't accept the gift, that it was too expensive, that when she used it she would think of him and be sad. In the end she took it because she wanted the reminder of their time together, this stolen week that she would never have again.

Though things between them were far from settled and would no doubt remain so even after he left Mistletoe, she had needed the break from her routine, and time with the man who'd seen that need and taken her away. The man she was quite sure she was coming to love.

She'd been thinking about her fast-growing feelings for him and whether or not she could trust them to be real. Of course they were heat-of-the-moment. Of course they were thrilling. Of course they were causing her a lot of sleepless nights.

But just because she was reveling in the excitement of what she was feeling didn't mean she'd lost her ability to distinguish between reality and fiction.

Fiction was the lies that had been printed about her life with Marshall. Reality was living through the resulting humiliation and being careful not to do anything, to say anything that would ruin the safe—if somewhat lonely—life she'd carved out for herself after the end of her other one.

She knew that, but she also knew she had to tell Caleb the truth about who she was if she wanted what they had found here to grow. They had just sat down for their second meal of their day away in Golden when she made the decision to do so. Once they'd finished here they'd be driving back, and she didn't want to have this conversation in the dark with both of them facing the road any more than she'd wanted to have it in bed.

The booth in which they were sitting in the casual restaurant offered just enough privacy. She reached for the margarita their server set in front of her, and once Caleb had his beer, she took a deep breath, found her courage, and began.

"Did I tell you that I was born in Mistletoe? Even went to business school at the University of Colorado in Denver and majored in marketing? My parents both worked for the school district before retiring to Arizona."

"Hmm. But you lived out of state before moving to Colorado."

"Right. I left here not long after graduation to work for an ad agency on the East Coast." She paused, returned her glass to the table and added, "In Baltimore."

Caleb's gaze came up. He'd been studying his menu,

drinking his beer, but with those two words, she had his full attention. "You were living there before I moved there then."

She nodded. "And you were there when I moved away."

She left her admission at that for the moment, reaching again for her drink which she knew wasn't going to be enough to get her through their meal. She was tense, stiff, frightened. She was about to give up her safety net to a man who had never promised to catch her.

Caleb, who had been leaning forward, suddenly sat back as if pinned to his seat by a blast. His eyes went wide. The expression on his face was the shock of a man poleaxed. "Gordon. You were married to E. Marshall Gordon. You were Miranda Gordon."

Just as she'd thought. He knew exactly who she was. "Maybe say it one more time to be sure?"

"Oh, I'm sure," Caleb said, shifting forward again, shaking his head as if to help his suppositions fall into place. "That first night in Club Crimson, I knew I'd seen you, or at least that I should've known you, but I never could put it together. You…distracted me."

"In a good way, I hope," she said, toying with the stem of her glass.

"Considering I never let anything distract me…"

"I'll take that as a yes," she said, even though she could see that he was distracted now. He was blinking rapidly, giving her no more than a weak smile before getting back to whatever destination his mind was racing toward. "Caleb?"

"Hmm?"

"Caleb?"

He shook free from his thought-filled daze and reached for his beer. "Sorry. I was—"

"Lost in thought. Weighing the implications of me handing

you such a scoop and the ramifications of using it. Especially now, with Marshall's new trial coming up and speculation about what happened to me no doubt running rampant."

"I have heard of a renewed interest in finding you."

She pulled her drink closer. "I know. And I knew that's what you would do once you figured it out. At least I hoped that's what you would do. That you would think about it for a while."

He waited as a laughing foursome walked by their table. "Instead of pulling out my phone and e-mailing my editor, you mean?"

She nodded. "Or writing the headline before you knew the whole story."

"Does that mean you have more to tell me? Or more you want me to know? Because you've told me a lot, and I'm pretty good at cobbling all those different parts into something—"

"Big and juicy and guaranteed to make you a name?"

"Something like that," he said, but he looked away as if there was something he was holding back from her. A big juicy something he didn't want her to know.

She canted her head to the side and considered him as someone with a secret of his own. "So? What do you want to ask me? What are you curious about?"

This time, he was the one who considered her, frowning as if he didn't understand what she was asking. "I'm curious about all of it, but I didn't think you wanted me digging around."

"I don't. But I'm offering the information freely," she said just as their server returned to take their order. She went with a Cobb salad. Caleb chose a gourmet burger and home fries.

They both ordered a second drink and once the waiter gathered up their menus with a promise to be right back, they were left staring at one another across a table that seemed a whole lot wider than before.

Caleb was the first to speak. "I'm not so sure about that freely thing. I don't think those wounds are healed. I think if I started asking about what I want to know, you would bleed."

"That's ridiculous." Why would he think such a thing? "I've moved beyond all of that. It's ancient history."

"It's not that ancient. And moving to another state doesn't mean moving beyond. It's still there, Miranda. It's why you hate what I do. It's why you don't want the media connecting Miranda to Candy. Especially now. It's part of who you are. And it's why I think I—" He stopped in the middle of his sentence, reached for his mug and drained his beer.

Miranda didn't know how to react. Their server arrived with their second round of drinks, giving her a bit of breathing room. What had Caleb been about to say? That he loved her? That he enjoyed her company? That he had to leave Mistletoe before he got in too deep?

She could hardly believe it was any of those, and yet… "It's why you think you what?"

"It's why I never did put a lot of effort into finding out who you were. I like who you *are*. You said you'd tell me when it was time. And now…" He reached for the stack of coasters on their table, and tapped them on the tabletop the way he would a deck of cards.

"And now you wish I hadn't told you?"

"Yeah. In a way," he admitted, avoiding her gaze. "I mean, me liking you doesn't change the fact that I'm an entertainment correspondent."

"And now that Miranda Gordon is once again in the news

as scandal fodder…" She brought her drink to her mouth, swallowed, licked the salt from her lips. "Since I'm not a private citizen but a public figure and newsworthy, you've got to decide how to handle what I've told you."

"What do you want me to do with it?" he asked. "You had a reason for telling me. You had to have thought about what I'd do with the information."

"I wondered how you'd react, yes. Whether you'd rush off to make a call to meet a deadline."

"That's all? No other scenario?" he asked, cutting his gaze upward.

"Such as?"

"That I would respect your wishes and keep what you told me in confidence?"

She wondered—if she made that request, would he give her his word? "I guess not. I know your type. And I knew by telling you, that I was risking the information leaking out."

"And if it did, if I leaked it, were you going to leave Mistletoe and remake yourself somewhere else?"

That question was one she had no trouble answering, and she shook her head. "No. I'm staying where I am. I have friends, a business, my singing gig. I have a wonderful life."

"What about having Miranda Gordon's picture showing up in the paper next to Candy Cane's?"

She waited for the server to set their meals in front of them, reaching for her fork before going on. "If my name ends up in the paper, I'll deal with the fallout then. And if I'm lucky, people will still call me when they want flowers. If not, well, I'll cross that bridge when I come to it. Honestly, I'm more worried about Corinne."

He took a bite of his burger, studying her while he chewed and swallowed. "How so?"

Miranda realized she was going to have to walk a fine line between giving him her thoughts and giving him a lecture. She was pretty sure he wouldn't go for the latter. "I'm saying that gossip is damaging to more people than those it's about."

He nodded, but it wasn't a sign of agreement. That was obvious from the tightness of his mouth, the hard line of his jaw. "So if I write about you being in Mistletoe, it could hurt your business and take out Corinne as collateral damage. Is that what you're saying?"

He was close, and she expounded. "And if I were forced to sell or close the shop and Corinne were forced to find another job, it could impact Zoe's scholarship, especially if they had to move away for Corinne to get work. Mistletoe's not exactly a town with a lot of prospects."

"What would you do? If you had to leave?"

There was something she wanted to know before she answered. "Is my response going to influence what you do with my revelation?"

"Why did you tell me?" he asked, rather than giving her an answer. "You didn't have to. I didn't ask you to."

"You haven't for a couple of days, no."

"Then why? Knowing what you do about me—"

"What *do* I know about you, Caleb? That you're an entertainment correspondent writing a book. That's not a lot. I don't know if you have a column in *People* magazine or if you write for *TMZ*."

He looked down, grabbed a thick French fry and swirled it through a pool of ketchup. "I do have a column. It's syndicated. Nationally. Just not under my name."

And things just got better and better. "So you have a Candy Cane persona of your own?"

"More or less, yeah."

"And what would happen if I exposed you?"

"Do you know who I am?"

She shook her head. Until now, she hadn't thought he was anyone with an alter ego she might recognize. "No, but I know how to use Google. I also know a couple of private investigators who would love to hear from me again."

He sat back, ran his napkin over his mouth and tossed it to the table before reaching for his mug and draining it. "What do you want me to do with the information, Miranda? Sit on it? Write about it? Give it to the Baltimore press?"

"I want you to add it to what you already know about me and see if it changes anything."

"Such as?"

"Your feelings," she blurted out, because right now that was the only thing that mattered to her. She ached with wanting him, loving him, needing to know he shared the incredible high she'd been riding this past week.

He obviously didn't. "I'm not much for feelings."

"Then you're lucky that you can push them aside," she said, tossing her napkin to the table. "Most of us aren't able to do that so easily."

"It's not about pushing them aside."

"Then what is it?"

"I can only do what I do, the type of reporting I do, by keeping my distance. I can't get personally involved. Things get…fucked up when I do."

"With me, you mean."

"With anyone."

"Then thank God I didn't tell you how I really feel," she said, scooting to the end of the bench seat and getting to her feet before they shook out from under her. "I'm going to the ladies' room. Could you settle the check so we can go?"

THE DRIVE BACK WAS MADE in absolute darkness and silence. Caleb didn't want to leave things with Miranda any worse than he sensed they were, and figured his best shot at doing that was shutting the hell up.

He'd come so close to telling her that he loved her. He'd almost blurted it out in the middle of their conversation. Judging by the look on her face, he was pretty sure she knew he'd caught himself in the nick of time.

And then he'd compounded the error by denying he felt anything at all. Such a smart guy he was. Such a brilliant piece of work.

Funny thing was, he'd been ready to tell her that no woman had ever meant to him what she did, that he woke up in the mornings wanting her there, that when he thought about their time together, the simplest things made him smile, that their knowing each other only a matter of days made no difference at all.

The look on her face when she'd caught him ordering her flowers. The way she'd taken over the inn's kitchen the night they'd sneaked in for a snack. Her leaving him to discover the only way to get from the warehouse to his room was to trek outside the building through the cold and the snow.

All of those things—and others, dozens of others—were at the heart of his inability to get his work done and get out of here, and he didn't even care. Leaving tomorrow was eating at him. Unbelievably so.

He could see himself sticking around, bunking in with Miranda, working on his book on the sofa or the kitchen island, while she curled up beside him to read or put a pot of coffee on.

He'd been having thoughts of home and hearth…and then she'd dropped her Baltimore bomb into his lap. He had no idea what he was going to do with it.

The Caleb he'd been a month ago, before the fiasco with Del's fiancée, would've done the very thing she'd wondered about, pulled out his cell phone and e-mailed his editor a sound bite for WBAL-TV's evening news.

The Caleb he was now, the one who found himself seriously considering a recent offer to buy his Max Savage empire, that Caleb was fighting a battle between his feelings for Miranda and the power trip of telling all.

"What did you say?"

At Miranda's question, he glanced over, seeing nothing but her profile lit by the glowing dashboard lights. "Did I say something?"

She nodded. "It sounded like a curse."

"It probably was."

"What were you thinking?"

He wasn't going to tell her that. Once he figured out what he was going to do, he'd let her know, whichever way it went, but he wasn't going to talk about it now. Instead, he turned to something that was still weighing on his mind.

"About work. About reporting. About the stories we hear, how much we never know of what's behind them."

"But it's that way with all news. Not just celebrity gossip. In cases of national security, we're given what the reporters and correspondents are allowed to make public. It's the same with the criminal justice system, or even human-interest stories. We may hear about someone losing two hundred pounds, but we don't know if it was really done for health reasons or because their spouse threatened to leave."

"Doesn't say much about the spouse, does it?" he responded without really thinking.

"I was speaking hypothetically, but, no. A lot of couples do fine through the better, but fall apart through the worse."

They weren't officially a couple, but they had come to a better-or-worse crossroads. What he did with her story would determine whether he'd be welcome in Mistletoe, whether he'd switch his home base from Maryland to Colorado, or whether he'd never see Miranda Kelly again.

That was Caleb's final thought as he pulled the borrowed SUV to a stop in front of her bungalow. He left the engine idling, but neither one of them made a move to get out. This could be the last time they ever saw one another, both of them knew that, and he was gripped by a sadness that was hard to shake.

"Do you want to stay the night?" she finally asked.

"I do, but I can't. I have to pack, and Barry's meeting me in front of the inn at four-thirty. My flight leaves at seven."

"Gotta love all that airport security adding hours to the process," she said, and they laughed together awkwardly.

Miranda took a deep breath. "This is goodbye then."

"Only for now."

"Does that mean you're coming back?"

"That means we'll see. I've got some things to do, to work on. Things to think about."

"The book?"

"Yeah. There's that."

"And what I told you."

"There's that, too."

She opened her door then, so Caleb did the same, retrieving her overnighter from the backseat once he'd climbed out. He circled the vehicle to walk her to her door. She was already halfway up the walk when he got to her side, so he did the only thing he could do and followed.

She dug in her purse for her keys, unlocked the door. He pushed it open far enough to set her luggage inside, but stayed on the porch, feeling that he'd worn out his welcome over the dinner neither one of them had eaten much of.

"Thank you for the day away," Miranda said, turning up her face and meeting his gaze. "I can't remember the last time I had so much fun. And it was even better with you there to share it."

"I had a great time, too," he said, knowing he had to go, that there was nothing to be gained by standing here telling her goodbye in a dozen different ways when there was only one way he wanted to say it.

He stepped closer, brought up his hand to cup her face, guided her close to his body with his other one in the small of her back and kissed her. It was a tentative, questing kiss, a gentle pressing together of their lips, of hers parting, of his tongue slipping inside to find hers.

He knew she was crying before he heard the hitch in her breathing and felt her tremble against him. Hot tears ran down her cheeks and wet his. He tasted their saltiness, used his thumb to wipe away what he could reach. She curled her fingers against his chest, holding on to the fabric of his sweater.

That was when she pulled away. "Where is your coat? Aren't you freezing?"

If he was, he hadn't noticed. "I'm fine. The heater's on in the SUV."

"I guess you'd better get back to the inn so Alan doesn't have to walk home."

"Yeah. I guess I'd better."

"Thank you again. For the minibreak."

"Thank you," he said, wondering if he was about to have a heart attack, his chest hurt so bad. "For everything."

# *21*

MIRANDA HAD NEVER HATED a Monday morning more. She got up, got dressed, skipped breakfast and got to work early, and did it all without having slept during the night.

She'd tried. Over and over, she'd tried. But she'd tossed and turned, paced from the bedroom to the kitchen and back fifteen times, finally sitting in the hot shower until her water heater spat out its last drop of warmth.

A prune by then, she'd given up the bed and built a fire, then curled up on the couch and nursed a mug of soothing herbal tea that hadn't done such a good job of soothing. She didn't blame the tea. She was beyond being soothed.

She'd had an amazing six days with Caleb—six days that seemed like six weeks, six months even, but it was over. He was gone, and he'd taken her secret with him back to the very city where her life had fallen apart. Now all she could do was sit here in her hideaway and wait for the backlash.

When four o'clock had rolled around, she'd thought about calling him before he left and asking him if he'd decided what to do with the news. She hadn't, her pride rising up and smacking her before she could make that mistake.

She'd chosen to tell him the truth of her identity, now she had to face the consequences of her actions. That meant she had to go to work without having slept a wink. And for the first time in a long while, she beat Corinne to the shop.

The other woman stopped inside the back door, looked at her watch, looked up at Miranda where she stood at the worktable sorting carnations. "Am I in the right place?"

Miranda scowled. "You, mother of the bride. Don't try to be funny. I'm not in a funny mood."

"Well, you're in some kind of mood." Corinne tucked her purse in her locker and pulled her apron over her head, looking cheerier and younger than she had in ages. "Couldn't have anything to do with the love of your life leaving town, could it?"

"He was not, is not, will never be the love of my life. He was just…a guy," Miranda said, cringing inside at how false her statement sounded, how wrong it felt. "We got back from Golden pretty late, and I didn't sleep, and here I am, grumpy and tired."

"Go home. Take a nap," Corinne suggested, checking the order book for what needed doing first, finding the season's usual requests for poinsettias and the like. "There's nothing going on that I who have no worries and a wonderful new son-in-law can't handle."

As happy as she was for Corinne, Miranda couldn't stand the thought of being alone the day Caleb was leaving town. "If I go home, I'll pace and fret like I did all night."

"And you'd rather do that here. Inflict your pain on an audience."

Miranda threaded her fingers into her hair, took a deep breath, and forced it out loudly. "No pain. No inflicting. I promise."

"He's not such a bad guy, you know. For a reporter," Corinne said, heading to the bathroom to wash her hands while Miranda stared at her aghast.

"And you're telling me that now because…"

"He wasn't sticking around." Corinne shook the water from her hands before pulling three paper towels from the dispenser. "Does it matter when I gave you my opinion?"

"It's not the same opinion you gave me when you found out what he does."

"That's why they're called opinions," Corinne said, patting Miranda's shoulder as she walked by on her way to the front of the store. "They're subject to change."

"And what changed yours?" Miranda called before Corinne disappeared from the back room.

She stopped in the arched walk-through. "I spent some time with him on Saturday, before the wedding. He's got a good heart. Good intentions. He made doubly sure that he got everything about Brenna's story right."

"Are you saying he's one of a few good newsmen? A reporter who knows where to draw the line?"

"He stepped over a time or two, but was a good sport when I pushed him back."

"Then maybe I don't have to worry about the Baltimore press descending like the plague?"

The front door opened then, putting an end to her musings and their conversation. Since she wasn't getting much of anything done, she followed Corinne to the front.

It was Orsy from next door with a box of donuts in one hand and an envelope in the other. Orsy always offered his neighbors freebies when they came in, but he never delivered.

"Hey, Orsy." Miranda leaned her elbows on the front counter. "Is it a special occasion? Or are you just teasing me before you take those somewhere else?"

The bakery owner laughed as he set the box in front of her. "Nope. These are for you. Guy who came in last week and wanted the sausage biscuits told me to bring 'em over when you and Corinne got in."

"Caleb?" she asked, knowing the answer, her heart racing, her thoughts speeding ahead.

"Didn't give a name. Had Barry drop him by first thing. Did give me this, though. Asked that I made sure you got it." Orsy handed her the envelope, before turning for the door. "You ladies have a good day."

"Thanks, Orsy. You, too," Miranda said, glancing over at Corinne. "Donut?"

"I think I will," the other woman said, opening the box. "What's in the envelope?"

"A Dear Jane letter, I'd imagine." She wasn't about to admit that her stomach was in knots. She was having enough trouble hiding the tremors in her hands.

"So open it already," Corinne said, gesturing with her donut and dropping sugar crumbs everywhere. "See what the reporter has to say."

Miranda reached for a letter opener and slit the top. A strip of newspaper fluttered out to land on the counter. It was the most recent Max Savage column. And it was signed.

"Oh my God! Your reporter is Max Savage!" Corinne grabbed the article away from Miranda. "And look here. He says he'll be doing a weeklong feature on the newly married Ravyn Black and Teddy Eagleton."

Miranda couldn't even think about Corinne's daughter. Caleb was Max Savage! The Snoop with the Scoop! Dear God, the man had the ability to smear her from here to Baltimore and around the world.

The question was, would he? Or had he already? Was her name slated to appear in tomorrow's column?

She leaned her elbows on the counter and buried her face

in her hands. Max Savage. She never would have imagined things would turn out this bad.

"Hey, he wrote you a note. Here. On the back." Corinne stabbed a finger against the newspaper.

Miranda hadn't seen it. All she'd seen was the heavy black signature scratched above the column's headline.

She picked up the paper and turned it over, unable to groan or laugh, afraid she was going to throw up. She was screwed. So incredibly screwed.

And then she read what Caleb had written…

You were honest with me. This may be a chickenshit way of returning the favor, but never let it be said that I wasn't an honest chickenshit.
Caleb

"Well, there ya go," Corinne said. "Can you believe it? You were sleeping with Max Savage. What a hoot! Now if he tells the world who you are, you can out him back."

Somehow, that didn't make Miranda feel any better. Right now, she didn't think there was anything that would.

CALEB'S FLIGHT FROM Denver to Baltimore was amazingly uneventful and even on time. If he was a suspicious man, he would've taken that as a sign that he was meant to forget Mistletoe and Miranda, and reclaim his life from the strange week he'd spent at the Inn at Snow Falls. But it wasn't going to happen, and he knew it.

He would always remember the redhead he'd found living on the mountain. The redhead he'd fallen in love with.

Leaving her his most recent column on his way out of town hadn't exactly been a fair way to tell her who he was—not when she'd come out to him twice, first as Candy Cane, then about being the ex-Mrs. E. Marshall Gordon.

All he'd done was sign a newspaper. Not hard to figure out which one of them had the balls. At least Barry's chatter during the drive to the airport had distracted him from thoughts of further professional hara-kari.

Once he was in the air, he'd pulled out his laptop and his earbuds, plugged in and tuned out everyone else on the plane. He'd spent the flight looking over the notes for the week's worth of columns he'd drafted about the romance of the congressman and the rock star, then pulled up a new document to put down random thoughts on his book.

It hadn't been easy deciding how to start the study of his observations on the tabloids and society until he'd realized that his own decade spent reporting entertainment news, and the impact doing so had had on him, would make a perfect preface. Yeah, he'd be putting himself out there as Max Savage, but it was time to own his mistakes as well as his successes. He had a lot of both. He was proud of the bulk of it, but not all.

While crossing the continent at thirty thousand feet, he'd discovered his story wasn't particularly difficult to chronicle. By the time the plane began its descent into BWI, he had the first draft of the preface polished within an inch of its life.

He shut down his laptop, grabbed his computer bag and his carry-on and disembarked, heading to the cab stand. He gave the driver his address, then settled back for the trip to his town house, his brain engaged with where he'd be picking up in the book once he was home.

He'd need food delivered, coffee, milk and cereal to see him from one Chinese takeout to the next. But this felt right, this buckling down and digging in to get it done. It needed to be said, to be shared, to serve as a warning or a lesson, or, hell, even as entertainment to those who would take it that way. And when he *was* done, when he'd bled the words he wanted to say all over the page, he'd send it to his agent and to Miranda.

He wanted her to know what he had written. But most of all he wanted her to know that he loved her, and that if she couldn't love him back because of who he was, what he had done, the things he stood for, he'd live with that.

And with Max Savage being laid to rest, neither she nor anyone else would have to suffer his bite again.

# 22

MIRANDA WAS IN NO MOOD to go onstage. She'd thought about calling in sick this last week of December, coming back after the new year was well under way with a new attitude and list of resolutions and goals.

But this week was the busiest of the year at the Inn at Snow Falls, and she had too much pride in the reputation of Club Crimson and too much love for Candy Cane to bail on the show and her friends.

The new year would be here soon enough, along with the whole new outlook on life she was determined to have. There would be no more hiding and worrying about being found out. If she wanted to fly to Baltimore and visit old friends, fly to Baltimore she would.

She'd done enough waiting around like a lump on a log and hoping for things to happen this past month, waiting for Caleb to get in touch, hoping he would call and tell her what he had decided to do with what she'd told him about who she was.

Hoping more for him to call and say that he missed her. That he loved her. And then she realized how much time and energy she was wasting with her passivity, and she'd given herself a lecture that was long overdue.

No, from now on, whatever she wanted or hoped for, she

would go after. She was done with hiding, done thinking privacy and anonymity would protect her from the ugly things said by people who didn't know her.

Cloistering herself away in a small mountain town was not going to stop the gossip any more than had keeping a low profile while living in the city. People who wanted to talk and speculate were going to talk and speculate.

All she could do was hold her head high and go on living her life. And that meant letting what she'd shared with Caleb fade into a wonderful memory, no matter how painful that was for her to admit.

His parting *we'll see* had obviously been his way of letting her down easy, when telling her he'd enjoyed the week for what it was would've been a much kinder kiss-off.

Sure, she could've called him. She didn't know if he was listed, but her contacts in Baltimore would've had no trouble finding him—once they got over the shock of hearing from her. But the thought of chasing him down after leaving the ball in his court seemed so…desperate.

Sitting on the vanity bench in her dressing room, she stared at her reflection. Before Caleb McGregor had come into her life, she'd experienced bouts of loneliness, had griped to Corinne and Patrice about the lack of eligible men in Mistletoe until her friends had tired of hearing her whine.

But she'd never let herself fall into a pit of desperation or depression. The fact that she was so close to doing so now—

"Miranda? You in there?"

At Patrice's voice, Miranda turned from facing herself to facing the rest of the world. "It's unlocked," she called, reaching for the band that held back her hair. "Come in."

Patrice opened the door. "I knocked, like, three times. I guess you were in the bathroom."

"No, I was here. Thinking. I didn't hear you, sorry."

"I'd ask what you were thinking about, but since Caleb has been the only thing on your mind lately…" Patrice let the sentence trail off as she perched beside Miranda on the bench. "Maybe this will help."

She handed Miranda a manila envelope addressed to her with nothing in the upper left corner but a block-printed CM. There was no postmark to show that it had come from Baltimore. In fact, there were no stamps at all.

She touched her fingertips to the initials, her pulse quickening. "Is he here?"

"Not that I know of," Patrice said, stabbing the center of the envelope with one finger. "I'm assuming that came with the rest of today's FedEx packages. Alan said he tried to flag you down when you came in—"

He had. She'd ignored him. "I heard him. I was too busy having a pity party to want to talk."

"Aw, sweetie." Patrice wrapped an arm around Miranda's shoulders. "What's the pity for this time?"

Miranda elbowed her friend in the ribs. "This time? Just for that, I'm not telling you."

"You don't have to tell me. It's written all over your face."

Miranda looked up to check her reflection. "I see a frown that's easily remedied with a smile, and some under-eye circles that I'll need makeup to get rid of. But nothing written there except my lack of sleep."

"You know what I see when I look at you?" Patrice took the large envelope from Miranda's hands and held it up. "I see this. Him. You're in love with the man and you're not doing anything about it."

"What am I supposed to do?" Miranda asked, flailing one hand. "He told me he'd be in touch, and he hasn't been."

Patrice waved the envelope. "What do you call this?"

Hmph. "A month late?"

"He's a guy, Miranda. A month of sorting out his feelings is nothing."

Miranda stared at the packet. She was certain it contained the decision he'd made in one form or another. What she couldn't figure out was why he thought she would want to read about it this way rather than hearing it firsthand.

Patrice patted at the envelope. It was almost a half-inch thick, and stiff, as if it held cardboard. "Aren't you at all curious?"

"Of course I'm curious."

"Well, then? Open it and see what he has to say," Patrice said, peeling back the adhesive flap to get Miranda started.

Miranda took it from there, sliding out a small sheaf of three-holed paper bound together with metal fasteners. A handwritten note was paper-clipped on top.

The opening to my book.
I wanted you to be the first to read it.
Caleb

"Ooh," Patrice said. "I've never been able to resist a sneak peek."

"If this is what I think it is, he's written about me," Miranda said, even though she couldn't figure out why Caleb would put her in a book about pop culture. It didn't make sense, but why else would he send it?

Patrice was quiet for several seconds, then said, "Maybe you shouldn't read it until after the show then."

"No, I have to know what it says."

"Do you want me to flip through and give you the highlights?"

Miranda shook her head. She was going to be strong. Nothing he had written could hurt her, whether a lie or the truth. "Why don't you read it to me while I do my face?"

Patrice gave her one more chance to back out. "You sure you don't want to look at it while you're alone?"

"So I can have an even bigger pity party?"

"If you're sure…"

Miranda nodded. She wasn't sure at all. "I am."

"Okay." Patrice opened the cover page to read.

In 1995, Caleb McGregor graduated from the Newhouse School of Public Communications at Syracuse University. Having interned at the *New York Times* in his senior year, he was ready to find and report "all the news that was fit to print"—as stated in the logo found in the paper's masthead. Things didn't go as planned, and several years later he discovered his true calling, reinventing himself as Max Savage.

All he had to do was play Faust to Max's devil, and he had a guaranteed ride to the top. He was arrogant. He was impatient. He was greedy beyond belief. And so, like the brash and impatient young fool that he was, he sold his soul and said yes, digging into the lives of celebrities, politicians, society's movers and shakers, and feeding their stories to a public starved for his brand of news.

Patrice stopped, and met Miranda's gaze in the vanity mirror. "Sweetie, I'm not so sure this is about you at all."

"Let me see it." Miranda flipped through the pages, reading tidbit after vignette after recountal about Caleb, and not a word about Miranda Gordon or Candy Cane. She looked back up at Patrice. "This isn't about me. It's about him."

"Why him?"

"He's Max Savage."

Patrice's eyes went wide. "The gossip columnist? You've got to be kidding me."

Miranda shook her head. It had been a month since she'd received the signed column at the flower shop, but she hadn't breathed a word to anyone else, and knew Corinne would never repeat what she'd been told in confidence.

"He told me with a note after he left."

"And you didn't spill?"

"I didn't think he wanted it known."

"Well, if this is the opening to his book, I'd guess that he's changed his mind. I wonder why."

Miranda was wondering, too. "Listen, do you mind if I read the rest of this alone?"

"Sure, sweetie." Patrice dropped a kiss on the top of Miranda's head as she stood. "I know where I'm not wanted just the same as I know where I am wanted. I've got a hot date with an even hotter bartender."

"I was wondering what was up with the shoes," Miranda said, glancing down to the low-heeled pumps Patrice had coordinated with dress pants instead of wearing her usual blue jeans and boots.

"We're going out to dinner at Fish and Cow Chips, if you can believe it," Patrice said, waving goodbye as she opened the door, then nodding to indicate the manuscript pages. "You'll let me know what he says?"

"Of course. I just need to get through it on my own first."

"Okay, but don't forget you go on in an hour."

"Yes, Mrs. Club Manager. I'll be on time."

And then Patrice was gone, the door closing behind her, and Miranda was left with Caleb's story and the realization that he hadn't written his pièce de résistance about her. Had it been arrogant of her to think that was what he was going to do?

She looked at the top of the last sheet, saw that there were only fifty pages. She had an hour and would be cutting it close, but she didn't care.

She started at the beginning and read through to the end, seeing in his words so much of the Caleb she'd come to know, learning things about him she hadn't had time to find out in their six days together. Discovering what a complicated man she'd fallen in love with. Accepting that anyone wishing to make a life with him would have her work cut out.

He was not an easy man, a simple man. He was full of complexities and contradictions; she knew from her experience that he was set on things going his way.

And then she turned the last page, and she found a note that wasn't meant for his agent or editor or the scandal-loving public. It was meant only for her.

And it made her smile as her heart began to thump with a new beat in her chest.

You owe me an end-of-show kiss.

# 23

I T HAD TAKEN CALEB a long time to figure out how to pull off the biggest romantic gesture he'd ever made in his life. The only one he'd ever made, if he were being honest.

And since it was time to be honest about everything, well, yeah. He'd never done anything like this before, or even had the desire or the need—until he'd been smart enough to fall in love with Miranda Kelly.

The day Caleb had left Mistletoe and flown out of Colorado, he'd tipped Orsy well enough that he had no doubt the baker had delivered the donuts and the signed Max Savage column to Miranda at Under the Mistletoe.

Now it was almost the new year—meaning Miranda had had almost a month to deal with Caleb being Max. The same month Caleb had used to exorcise his alter ego from his life.

He'd had to do it. He had to be free before he returned to grovel for Miranda's forgiveness, and beg her to share the rest of his life.

His first romantic gesture had been to call the flower shop and talk to Corinne. Fortunately, he'd only had to hang up on Miranda twice before her employee had answered the phone.

Corinne was good to play along and keep his plans to herself. He had no idea how she would fill his order without Miranda catching on, but that he left up to her.

Next he'd called the inn and talked to Alan. Caleb knew Club Crimson's manager was the best hope for pulling strings and getting him a room at the inn. He was also Caleb's best hope for a ride from the airport that would avoid using both Barry and the front door once he arrived.

Unfortunately, all Alan could provide was the ride; the inn was booked solid. Caleb had made the trip anyway. If things went well, he'd be sleeping with Miranda. If not, well, he'd bunked down in worse places than the inn's lobby while waiting to get out of one town or another.

He'd originally planned to overnight the section of the manuscript to Miranda. But he didn't want the pages arriving without him there to explain should his flight be delayed due to the holiday crush. So he'd tucked the FedEx envelope in his computer bag and given it to Alan after the other man had parked behind the inn in the employee's lot.

He'd also brought a copy of his final Max Savage column to show Miranda before it ran on New Year's Day. Signing off on the sale of Max Savage had been one of the sweetest moments of his life.

But nothing would compare to the moment when he laid eyes on Miranda again.

Walking into Club Crimson had been like walking into a rose garden. Dozens of the red flowers sat on every table in the nightclub save for one. His table. The one where he'd been sitting the first night he'd seen her.

Now he sat exactly where he had then.

Tonight, however, he was sober.

The glass in front of him contained nothing but water, ice and a slice of lime. He didn't need the clarity of mind to figure out who she was the way he had that first night. But neither did he need the crutch to get him beyond the hard-sell color scheme.

He still hated the red. He hadn't changed his mind about the whole concept of a lovers' resort as ridiculous. And if it hadn't been Miranda singing the songs, he wouldn't have stuck around for the sugary-sweet set.

But since it *was* Miranda, and he was involved on a level felt by no one else in the club, the moment the pianist began warming up, Caleb jumped in his seat, certain his heart was attacking for real.

It got worse when she came onstage. And it intensified as she sang, that feeling of his chest exploding, his lungs crushing him, his spine snapping as he broke. Through it all, she ignored him.

Not once did she look toward where she knew he would be sitting. Oh, no. She gave her attention to everyone else, stopped at every other table and leaned close to smell the flowers. His flowers. The flowers he'd had put there for her.

He bristled when she touched the men, grunted when she touched the women. He wanted her touching him. He wanted to be touching her. From the corner of his eye, he caught Alan at the bar gesturing his offer to break the rules and bring Caleb a real drink.

He came close to taking it, but that was when the opening notes to her final song floated through the club, and Miranda began walking toward him.

Not a single word of the lyrics registered. All he knew was that she was there, then on his table, draped across it as she sang, teasing him with flirtatious smiles, with the tip of her tongue as it wet her lips, with her teeth as she bit at the corner of the bottom one and caught it.

Her eyes teased him, too, tears glistening in the corners, the moisture reflecting the joy he saw there. The same joy he couldn't keep out of his own.

She straightened then, slid from the table into his lap, giving him a glimpse of both breasts as she moved and the scooped neckline of her sequined dress gaped.

And then she finished the song, drawing out the final note as she looped her arms around his neck, before whispering, "I love you," against his mouth, and kissing him.

He crushed her to him and kissed her back, not asking, not pleading, just sliding his tongue into her mouth the moment she parted her lips. Exquisite. Her taste. Her texture. The warmth of her mouth on his. The scent of flowers that was hers and had nothing to do with the roses.

He could not believe he had flown away and left her behind. He could not believe she was taking him back, that she was loving him, that she loved him, that she was going to let him love her. He didn't deserve her, but he was here for as long as she would have him.

Too soon, she pulled away, breathing deeply as if she'd forgotten she needed to. He knew breathing had slipped his own mind and he, too, inhaled, filling lungs that had finally remembered how to work.

When Miranda got to her feet and took a bow, the crowd around them clapped wildly.

Caleb also stood and, tears bright on her cheeks, Miranda reached up and laid her hand along his jaw. "I missed you."

"I doubt half as much as I missed you," he got out, his voice only cracking once. He suddenly couldn't see so well, his own eyes watery.

"We'll have to debate that later," she told him, stepping closer and pressing her body to his. "On our date."

He groaned. "Since I'm here without a room, I was hoping you'd say that."

She laughed, shook her head, then fluffed at her short auburn hair. "Did you notice I'm not wearing a wig?"

"I noticed. I also noticed you're not wearing a bra."

"That was just for you."

"Good. I'm a big fan of secrets."

"I was wondering about that," she said, and all he could do was drink her in as she added, "You know, not that I care so much anymore, but it's good to know you're not the kiss-and-tell type."

"Are you kidding me? Kissing and telling is what I do best." And before she could respond, he took her microphone, brought it to his mouth and stared into her shimmering eyes.

"I love you, too," he said, silently adding, "Miranda," before bending her backwards, following her down, and while the audience whooped and cheered, kissing her with every bit of that love.

* * * * * *

*Here is a sneak preview of*
*A STONE CREEK CHRISTMAS,*
*the latest in Linda Lael Miller's acclaimed*
McKETTRICK *series.*

A lonely horse brought vet Olivia O'Ballivan to Tanner
Quinn's farm, but it's the rancher's love that might cause
her to stay.

*A STONE CREEK CHRISTMAS,*
*available December 2008*
*from Silhouette Special Edition.*

Tanner heard the rig roll in around sunset. Smiling, he wandered to the window. Watched as Olivia O'Ballivan climbed out of her Suburban, flung one defiant glance toward the house and started for the barn, the golden retriever trotting along behind her.

Taking his coat and hat down from the peg next to the back door, he put them on and went outside. He was used to being alone, even liked it, but keeping company with Doc O'Ballivan, bristly though she sometimes was, would provide a welcome diversion.

He gave her time to reach the horse Butterpie's stall, then walked into the barn.

The golden retriever came to greet him, all wagging tail and melting brown eyes, and he bent to stroke her soft, sturdy back. "Hey, there, dog," he said.

Sure enough, Olivia was in the stall, brushing Butterpie down and talking to her in a soft, soothing voice that touched something private inside Tanner and made him want to turn on one heel and beat it back to the house.

He'd be damned if he'd do it, though.

This was *his* ranch, *his* barn. Well-intentioned as she was, *Olivia* was the trespasser here, not him.

"She's still very upset," Olivia told him, without turning to look at him or slowing down with the brush.

Shiloh, always an easy horse to get along with, stood contentedly in his own stall, munching away on the feed Tanner had given him earlier. Butterpie, he noted, hadn't touched her supper as far as he could tell.

"Do you know anything at all about horses, Mr. Quinn?" Olivia asked.

He leaned against the stall door, the way he had the day before, and grinned. He'd practically been raised on horseback; he and Tessa had grown up on their grandmother's farm in the Texas hill country, after their folks divorced and went their separate ways, both of them too busy to bother with a couple of kids. "A few things," he said. "And I mean to call you Olivia, so you might as well return the favor and address me by my first name."

He watched as she took that in, dealt with it, decided on an approach. He'd have to wait and see what that turned out to be, but he didn't mind. It was a pleasure just watching Olivia O'Ballivan grooming a horse.

"All right, *Tanner,*" she said. "This barn is a disgrace. When are you going to have the roof fixed? If it snows again, the hay will get wet and probably mold…"

He chuckled, shifted a little. He'd have a crew out there the following Monday morning to replace the roof and shore up the walls—he'd made the arrangements over a week before—but he felt no particular compunction to explain that. He was enjoying her ire too much; it made her color rise and her hair fly when she turned her head, and the faster breathing made her perfect breasts go up and down in an enticing rhythm. "What makes you so sure I'm a greenhorn?" he asked mildly, still leaning on the gate.

At last she looked straight at him, but she didn't move from Butterpie's side. "Your hat, your boots—that fancy red truck you drive. I'll bet it's customized."

Tanner grinned. Adjusted his hat. "Are you telling me real cowboys don't drive red trucks?"

"There are lots of trucks around here," she said. "Some of them are red, and some of them are new. And *all* of them are splattered with mud or manure or both."

"Maybe I ought to put in a car wash, then," he teased. "Sounds like there's a market for one. Might be a good investment."

She softened, though not significantly, and spared him a cautious half smile, full of questions she probably wouldn't ask. "There's a good car wash in Indian Rock," she informed him. "People go there. It's only forty miles."

"Oh," he said with just a hint of mockery. "*Only* forty miles. Well, then. Guess I'd better dirty up my truck if I want to be taken seriously in these here parts. Scuff up my boots a bit, too, and maybe stomp on my hat a couple of times."

Her cheeks went a fetching shade of pink. "You are twisting what I said," she told him, brushing Butterpie again, her touch gentle but sure. "I meant…"

Tanner envied that little horse. Wished he had a furry hide, so he'd need brushing, too.

"You *meant* that I'm not a real cowboy," he said. "And you could be right. I've spent a lot of time on construction sites over the past few years, or in meetings where a hat and boots wouldn't be appropriate. Instead of digging out my old gear, once I decided to take this job, I just bought new."

"I bet you don't even *have* any old gear," she challenged, but she was smiling, albeit cautiously, as though she might withdraw into a disapproving frown at any second.

He took off his hat, extended it to her. "Here," he teased. "Rub that around in the muck until it suits you."

She laughed, and the sound—well, it caused a powerful and wholly unexpected shift inside him. Scared the hell out of him and, paradoxically, made him yearn to hear it again.

\* \* \* \* \*

*Discover how this rugged rancher's wanderlust*
*is tamed in time for a merry Christmas, in*
*A STONE CREEK CHRISTMAS.*
*In stores December 2008.*

# SPECIAL EDITION™

## FROM *NEW YORK TIMES* BESTSELLING AUTHOR

# LINDA LAEL MILLER

## A STONE CREEK CHRISTMAS

Veterinarian Olivia O'Ballivan finds the animals in Stone Creek playing Cupid between her and Tanner Quinn. Even Tanner's daughter, Sophie, is eager to play matchmaker. With everyone conspiring against them and the holiday season fast approaching, Tanner and Olivia may just get everything they want for Christmas after all!

*Available December 2008
wherever books are sold.*

**SPECIAL EDITION**™

## MISTLETOE AND MIRACLES

by *USA TODAY* bestselling author
*MARIE FERRARELLA*

Child psychologist Trent Marlowe couldn't
believe his eyes when Laurel Greer, the
woman he'd loved and lost, came to him for
help. Now a widow, with a troubled boy who
wouldn't speak, Laurel needed a miracle from
Trent...and a brief detour under the mistletoe
wouldn't hurt, either.

*Available in December wherever books are sold.*

# THE ITALIAN'S BRIDE

Commanded—to be his wife!

Used to the finest food, clothes and women, these immensely powerful, incredibly good-looking and undeniably charismatic men have only one last need: a wife!

They've chosen their bride-to-be and they'll have her—willing or not!

**Enjoy all our fantastic stories in December:**

## THE ITALIAN BILLIONAIRE'S SECRET LOVE-CHILD
by CATHY WILLIAMS (Book #33)

## SICILIAN MILLIONAIRE, BOUGHT BRIDE
by CATHERINE SPENCER (Book #34)

## BEDDED AND WEDDED FOR REVENGE
by MELANIE MILBURNE (Book #35)

## THE ITALIAN'S UNWILLING WIFE
by KATHRYN ROSS (Book #36)

# HARLEQUIN® Romance®

## *Marry-Me Christmas*

by *USA TODAY* bestselling author

# SHIRLEY JUMP

A *Bride* FOR ALL *Seasons*

Ruthless and successful journalist Flynn never mixes business with pleasure. But when he's sent to write a scathing review of Samantha's bakery, her beauty and innocence catches him off guard. Has this small-town girl unlocked the city slicker's heart?

*Available December 2008.*

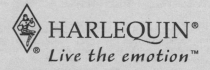

# HARLEQUIN®
## *Live the emotion*™

# REQUEST YOUR FREE BOOKS!

## 2 FREE NOVELS PLUS 2 FREE GIFTS!

HARLEQUIN®

*Blaze*™

**Red-hot reads!**

# THE MISTLETOE WAGER

## Christine Merrill

Harry Pennyngton, Earl of Anneslea,
is surprised when his estranged wife,
Helena, arrives home for Christmas.
Especially when she's intent on
divorce! A festive house party
Is in full swing when the guests
are snowed in, and Harry and
Helena find they are together
under the mistletoe....

*Available December 2008
wherever books are sold.*

# HARLEQUIN®
## Blaze™

# COMING NEXT MONTH

### #435 HEATING UP THE HOLIDAYS
### Jill Shalvis, Jacquie D'Alessandro, Jamie Sobrato
*A Hunky Holiday Collection*

Santa's finally figured out what women want—hot guys! And these three lucky ladies unwrap three of the hottest men around. Don't miss this Christmas anthology, guaranteed to live up to its title!

### #436 YULE BE MINE  Jennifer LaBrecque
*Forbidden Fantasies*

Journalist Giselle Randolph is looking forward to her upcoming assignment in Sedona…until she learns that her photographer is Sam McKendrick—the man she's lusted after for most of her life, the man she used to call her brother.…

### #437 COME TOY WITH ME  Cara Summers

Navy captain Dino Angelis might share a bit of his family's "sight," but even he never dreamed he'd be spending the holidays playing protector to sexy toy-store owner Cat McGuire. Or that he'd be fighting his desire to play with her himself…

### #438 WHO NEEDS MISTLETOE?  Kate Hoffmann
*24 Hours: Lost, Bk. 1*

Sophie Madigan hadn't intended to spend Christmas Eve flying rich boy Trey Shelton III around the South Pacific…or to make a crash landing. Still, now that she's got seriously sexy Trey all to herself for twenty-four hours, why not make it a Christmas to remember?

### #439 RESTLESS  Tori Carrington
*Indecent Proposals, Bk. 2*

Lawyer Lizzie Gilbred has always been a little too proper…until she meets hot guitarist Patrick Gauge. But even mind-blowing sex may not be enough for Lizzie to permanently let down her guard—or for Gauge to stick around.…

### #440 NO PEEKING…  Stephanie Bond
*Sex for Beginners, Bk. 3*

An old letter reminds Violet Summerlin that she'd dreamed about sex that was exciting, all-consuming, *dangerous!* And dreams were all they were…until her letter finds its way to sexy Dominick Burns…